THE SNATCH

THE SNATCH
by Bill Pronzini

A Foul Play Press Book
The Countryman Press, Woodstock, Vermont

This One Is for My Sister, Cathy, with Love

and

For Jeff Wallmann, the Other Half of the Gold Dust Twins

THE SNATCH

1

Tamarack Drive was one of these oak- and elm- and eucalyptus-shaded affairs that are supposed to make you think of rustic country lanes. There were no sidewalks on either side; instead, there were narrow creeks with mica rock beds and a trickle of water and root-tangled red-earth banks.

It was just past four in the afternoon when I parked my car behind a green panel truck that had the words *Burlingame Landscaping and Gardening Service* stenciled across its rear doors—and next to a post-supported mailbox crafted to represent a Lincolnesque log cabin, the numerals 416 in black iron extending like a billboard from its roof. Just beyond that, a narrow wooden footbridge spanned the creek to the front gate, and a larger wooden structure a little further on did the same to an interior drive; they were made out of redwood, with thick bark-covered railings and arched supports beneath to give the impression of tunneling. The gate was of redwood, too, set into a black wrought-iron frame, and so was the six-foot fence that stretched out on both sides. I could see the upper story of the house—a big modern Tudor with a gabled roof, set well back inside the grounds.

It was one of those warm, balmy autumn days, with just enough breeze to stir the fallen reddish-gold oak and elm leaves—the kind of day that makes you think of football games and long, leisurely strolls and pretty girls in short dresses with their hair blowing silken and free. I had the window rolled down, and the breeze was cool and soft against the side of my face; the aromatic scent of the eucalyptus was strong and pungent in the air.

I sat there for a time, watching the leaves flutter across asphalt patchworked with sunlight and shade. It was very quiet. This was Hillsborough, a sanctuary for the affluent and the snobbish on the Peninsula fifteen miles south of San Francisco, and when you entered its boundaries you stepped into a kind of Elysium where silence reigned supreme and noise of any kind constituted an unpardonable sin. I felt vaguely uncomfortable. I seemed always to feel that way in places like Hillsborough, the same feeling you might have if you found yourself at a formal party wearing slacks and a sport shirt.

I lit a cigarette, and that started the coughing again. I got out my handkerchief and covered my mouth with it. After a while the coughing stopped and I took the linen away and looked at it. There was a grayishness to the phlegm that made me shudder a little. I put the handkerchief in my pocket again and stabbed the cigarette into the ashtray and got out of the car.

I crossed the footbridge, and there was a small plaque fastened to the center of the redwood gate that said simply: *Martinetti*. On my right as I entered the grounds was a thick, green, well-trimmed lawn stretching away to a landscaped rock garden with a stone pond and a lot of evergreen shrubs and myrtle and spidery California wood ferns. The redwood fence extended in a right angle to form the boundary line along that side of the property, ending at another creek wider and deeper than the one bordering the street in front. The creek formed a natural rear boundary, and tall, slender eucalyptus trees grew along it in thick profusion. A young guy in a striped T-shirt and dungarees was kneeling on a spread piece of canvas nearby, weeding the lawn with a small trowel. He didn't look up as I entered.

There was more of the verdant lawn to the left, and beyond it a crushed gravel drive and a wide portico with room for three cars parked side by side. At the moment there were two: a new beige-colored Lincoln Continental and a ten-year-old immaculate MG roadster painted a gleaming silver. The lawn sloped into a raised terrace made of fieldstone, to the side of the house, and I could see the blue tile of an L-shaped swimming pool and a lot of heavy white wrought-iron patio furniture and an outdoor bar.

A white gravel path, inside very low stone retaining walls, curved up to the front door. I followed it, looking up at the house. I still had that vague feeling of discomfort I had known in the car.

A considerable amount of money had gone into the construction of the Martinetti home. It was huge and two-storied, fashioned of a mixture of brick and patterned stone and lavish half-timber work, with a big bay window along the one side overlooking terrace and pool. Rectangular mullioned windows were set on either side of the front door and on the facing second-story wall. Two high molded chimneys jutted upward on either side, advertising the presence of two sizable fireplaces within.

On the door was a heavy brass knocker in the shape of a lion's head; to lift it, you had to put your fingers inside the widespread jaws. I decided it was more decorative than functional. I found a small pearl button inlaid in the wood on one side and pressed that and listened to chimes, muted and rolling, echoing inside. I stood waiting, holding my hat in my hands.

Five seconds passed, and then the door opened and a thin girl with bright green, thick-lashed eyes looked out. She was in her early twenties, pretty in a gaunt sort of way. Her hair was cut short in what we used to call an Italian bob, and there was a white maid's cap perched precariously on the back of her head. A white peasant blouse and a dark skirt and flat-heeled shoes comprised her dress, and I supposed the silly little cap was to let you know that she was a servant and not a member of the household.

"Yes, sir?" she asked.

Before I could tell her who I was, and that I was expected, a tall dark-featured guy came up behind her and took the door gently out of her hands. He said, "It's all right, Cassy, I'll take care of it," and she nodded and disappeared obediently around him.

The guy took a step forward and looked me over noncommittally. He was about thirty, slender, gray-eyed, wearing a Roos/Atkins suit and a white shirt and a tasteful silver-and-blue tie. Black and cut short, his hair was carefully brushed in a way that was designed to minimize the size of his somewhat large ears. He seemed nervous and harried, and there were deep hollows in his cheeks that

6

might have gotten there from perpetual anxiety. He looked the ulcerous type.

He said, "Are you the detective Mr. Martinetti called?"

I said that I was.

"Well, please come in." He stood aside. "My name is Dean Proxmire. I'm Mr. Martinetti's secretary."

We shook hands, briefly. "How do you do?" I said, and felt foolish saying it. I wished I knew just how to handle myself in this kind of surroundings.

We were in a good-sized entrance hall, and there were a couple of pieces of decorative furniture on a muted broadloom carpet; several paintings in silver frames and a silver-framed antique mirror adorned the walls. Directly across from the door was a set of stairs leading up to a wrought-iron-railed balcony at the second floor. A wide doorway opened into a darkened living room, drapes drawn over the bay window, to the left of the stairs; to the right, an extension of the hall ran toward the rear of the house.

Proxmire took my hat and laid it carefully on the table under the mirror. He gestured toward the hall. "Mr. Martinetti and Mr. Channing are waiting in the study," he said.

I nodded, and we went down the hall and stopped before a set of carved double doors that looked as if they belonged in some baronial English manor. Proxmire tapped discreetly on the wood, and then opened one of the doors and stepped back so I could precede him inside.

The study was considerably longer than it was wide, redwood-paneled, with a beamed ceiling in a kind of diamond design. A large patterned-stone fireplace was set against the far wall, with staggered bookshelves flanking it and filling the near end wall; the mantelpiece and some of the shelves contained heavy hammered copper ewers and demijohns and the like. Next to the entrance doors on the left was a built-in stereo unit, and beyond that a recessed alcove that contained an impressive redwood-and-leather bar. The furnishings themselves were of the same style and materials: three thickly padded chairs, two long, low couches—one facing the fireplace; the other set before a massive oblong desk with a black leather executive's chair behind it—some heavy tables and a couple of mohair-shaded reading lamps. The desk was placed diagonally before the far left-hand corner, and dark brown damask drapes were drawn over windows extending the same distance on either side, forming a background V for the desk. It was very dark in there, and in spite of the appointments, I had the impression of austerity rather than solid masculine comfort, as if no one ever used this study simply to relax.

There were two men in the room, and both of them stood up as we came in. The man behind the desk was Louis Martinetti: tall, granite-hewn, hair and eyes the color of steel, nose strong and wide, the nostrils in a perpetual flare. He was forty-five, if you believed the newspapers, and from a distance he looked maybe ten years younger; you could almost feel the magnetism of the man reaching out at you across the room, and I was oddly reminded of an old pulp-magazine hero of the thirties and forties named Doc Savage. If Martinetti's face and hands had been bronzed instead of merely lightly tanned, his hair a metallic silver instead of dark gray, the resemblance might have been startling. He wore an old alpaca golfing sweater over a salmon-colored polo shirt, and beige doeskin slacks.

The other man, Allan Channing, was similarly dressed, but perhaps as sharp a physical contrast to Martinetti as you could imagine. He was big but not fat, with fine thinning hair the color, or non-color, of dust. He had pink cheeks and a soft mouth, and no particular magnetism at all. His eyes were wide and blue and innocent, containing the earnest guilelessness of an inquisitive child. Those eyes had fooled a lot of people over the years, and that was one of the reasons Channing was worth something like five or six million dollars at the last conservative press estimate.

They made a pretty awesome pair, Channing and Martinetti. They were speculators, angle boys, long-shot and sure-shot gamblers, wheelers-and-dealers. If you live in California, you know the type; it's a breeding ground for them. Real estate, industry, commerce—you name it, and if there's a dollar to be made from its exploitation, they'll find a way to make it. They were independents, self-made types, and if they had not been as adept, as cunning, as ruthless as they undoubtedly were, the large speculative concerns would have swallowed them up or destroyed them a long time ago.

Martinetti had made and lost a million dollars three or four times over the past twenty-odd years, and he had the reputation of being a hunch player who would take a flyer on almost anything if his judgment told him there was a chance it would pay off. Channing, on the other hand, was pretty much of a conservative; he liked to play it close to the vest, to leave the wildcatting to men like Martinetti. He had not come out on the short end in the past twenty years, and it was not likely that he ever would. That, in effect, was the difference between the two of them—and very possibly the reason that they had been able to remain friends over the years.

Proxmire and I approached the desk, and Martinetti's eyes appraised me with each step, running me through the snap-computer that was his mind, with no outward showing of conclusions. And as I neared him, I could see that something was bothering him, weighing heavily on his mind—and that whatever it was had cracked the granite of his physical being with a network of hairline fractures, like a solid substance about to fragment itself from some inner pressure. There was a gauntness to his face, a shadowed hollowness to the gray eyes. A tic had gotten up on the left side of his face, high on the cheekbone, and his full, expressive mouth was quirked oddly because of it.

Proxmire made the introductions, and I shook hands with Martinetti and then with Channing. There was a chair to one side of the desk, between it and the couch where Channing was, and I sat down there at Martinetti's indication and put my hands on my knees. He continued to stand behind his desk for a time, watching Proxmire retreat to the far end of the room but not out of it. Then, abruptly, he turned and walked across to the alcove where the bar was. He paused there, turning slightly, and said to me, "Would you care for a drink?"

"No, thank you," I answered.

"Allan?"

Channing shook his head. "Not just now, Lou." He seemed agitated, as if he found himself in a situation that he did not quite know how to cope with.

Martinetti poured four fingers of amber liquid from a decanter into a cut-crystal glass and returned to the desk. He sat down, and made a pyramid of his hands and rested his forehead on it for a long moment. Then he raised his head, looking directly at me.

"At ten o'clock this morning," he said, without preamble, "a man dressed in a dark-blue business suit and carrying a briefcase entered the headmaster's office at Sandhurst Military Academy in Burlingame. He introduced himself as a Mr. Edmonds, a member of the legal firm I employ, and showed a note written on my personal stationery to Mr. Young, the headmaster. The note said that Young was to release my son, Gary, to this Edmonds on a matter of the gravest personal importance. The note was ostensibly signed by me. Mr. Young summoned Gary from his class, and he and the man then left Sandhurst in a late-model station wagon."

Martinetti picked up his glass and drank from it. It was very quiet in the dark room—and suddenly very cold. "At two this afternoon, when Allan and I returned from a round of golf at the Burlingame Country Club, there was a telephone call for me," he went on. "A man's voice said that unless I paid him a specified amount of money, at a time and place of which I would later be notified, I could look for the body of my son in the Bay."

He was watching me intently now, waiting for my reaction. I avoided his eyes. I got out a cigarette and lit it and looked around for an ashtray. There were none. I put the match in my coat pocket. I could feel my lungs rebelling against the sharpness of the smoke, but the coughing did not start up again.

Martinetti said, "Do you understand what I've just told you? My son has been kidnapped."

"I understand it," I said. "Have you called the police yet?"

"No, and I don't intend to."

"Because of the threat?"

"That's right."

"They're still the people you want to talk to."

"No," Martinetti said. "I want my son back safely, and to get him back I'll follow any orders I'm given. No police."

"Just why did you call me, Mr. Martinetti?" I asked him. "I have neither the facilities nor the inclination to investigate a kidnapping."

"I don't want you to investigate anything," Martinetti said. There was an edge to his voice now, born of impatience and frustration and perhaps of fear.

"Then why?"

"The kidnapper wants a third party to make the money drop," he said slowly. "I don't know why. Maybe he's afraid if I do it myself, I'll panic or try something foolish. I don't know."

"How much do they want?"

He took a deep breath, held it, released it audibly. "Three hundred thousand dollars," he said.

I tapped some cigarette ash into the palm of my hand. The silence seemed to build in the room. I said finally, "What kind of arrangements were you given?"

"The bills are to be in small denominations, nothing larger than a hundred. I suppose that's standard procedure."

"It's the way this kind of thing is usually worked."

"I'm to put the money into a plain suitcase. Then I'm to wait for further instructions."

"Were you told when?"

"Tomorrow."

"But no particular time?"

"No."

12

I stared at a veined black marble pen set next to the telephone on his desk. I still could not meet his eyes. "Haven't you got someone here who can make the delivery for you? Mr. Channing, maybe, or—"

"I'm sorry," Channing said quickly from the couch. He had the kind of soft, sepulchral voice you come to expect from morticians. "Louis and I talked over that possibility, but I simply couldn't do it. I couldn't take that kind of responsibility."

No, I thought, but it's all right if I take it.

I said to Martinetti, "What about your secretary?"

He looked to where Proxmire was sitting on the couch in front of the fireplace. An odd, bitter little smile touched the corners of his mouth, and then disappeared as quickly as it had come. "I'm afraid not," he said.

"One of your other friends or business associates?"

"To be perfectly frank, there is no one I would care to trust with that kind of money."

"You're apparently prepared to trust me with it."

"You have a reputation for honesty, integrity and discretion in your profession. I made several reference calls before I telephoned you personally."

I did not say anything.

Martinetti said, "Will you do it?"

"I don't know."

"I'll pay you a thousand dollars."

"Listen, Mr. Martinetti . . ."

"Fifteen hundred, goddamn it! We're talking about my son's life here!"

I got up out of the chair and went over to the fireplace and threw my cigarette on the cordwood stacked in there. I dusted the ash off my hands, thinking that I didn't like it, I didn't like it at all. A kidnapping is a terrifying kind of thing—a cold, amoral, unnatural act—and in addition to leaving a bad taste in your mouth, the circumstances surrounding a crime of that nature are volatile enough so that you can never be sure what's going to happen next.

The police should have been notified immediately, in spite of the kidnapper's standard threat to the contrary; but I could understand Martinetti's hesitancy, and I did not blame him for wanting to keep the whole affair quiet—especially since he was a prominent enough figure in the area to rate considerable newspaper coverage if the story leaked out to the press. If I had been the father of an abducted child, I might have done things the same way. In any case, it was not my place to argue the propriety of paying a kidnap ransom demand, and certainly not the wisdom of it.

He had put me in a very uncomfortable position. If he had asked me to investigate the snatch of his son, I could have backed out without any qualms at all. And yet, all he had asked me to do was make the drop for him—just that, nothing else. With his mind made up to pay the three hundred thousand, somebody had to carry out the delivery; and the fewer people who knew about it, the better the boy's chances.

Fifteen hundred dollars. I had not had a client in five weeks, and fifteen hundred dollars was a considerable amount of money in my present state of affairs. But suppose I made a mistake? Suppose I fouled things up in some nebulous, unpredictable way, and something happened to Gary Martinetti? Suppose—?

Well, Jesus, suppose a hundred things, a thousand things. I got another cigarette out and lighted it, and then behind me Martinetti said in a voice stripped of all its normal power and magnetism, words that must have come very hard for a man like him, "Please. For God's sake—please."

I turned slowly. "All right," I said. "All right, Mr. Martinetti, I'll deliver the money for you."

2

Martinetti looked at me for perhaps five seconds, his face expressionless, and then he said, "Thank you, I—thank you," in a low voice and went over to the drapes and parted them and stood staring out broodingly.

I returned to my chair and sat down, conscious of the gazes of both Proxmire and Channing. I took a long drag on my cigarette, and one of the damned coughing attacks came on with no warning, violent and racking. By the time I got it under control, with the handkerchief to catch the phlegm, Martinetti was back at his desk. He was looking at me oddly.

"Are you all right?" he asked.

"Just a little chest cold," I said, even though I knew it wasn't. I did not want to talk about it. I went to the fireplace again and got rid of the butt and came back. Briefly, I wondered what the three of them in there were thinking about me; but it really was not important, and I put it out of my mind.

I said to Martinetti, "I'd like to know a few of the particulars of what happened today. I don't want to go into this completely cold."

He nodded. "What do you want to know?"

"To begin with, how many people know about the abduction?"

"The four of us in this room. My wife, Karyn, of course. I would imagine the maid, since she was about when the call came. And Young, the headmaster at Sandhurst."

"That's all?"

"Yes."

"Okay," I said. "How old is your son?"

"Nine."

"Bright?"

"Yes, very."

That wasn't necessarily a good thing, in circumstances such as these. Bright kids are generally perceptive of details, and a kidnapper would not want details related that might perhaps lead the authorities to him at some future time. I did not tell Martinetti that.

I said, "Are you in the habit of summoning him from school with a note, or by your lawyer?"

"No, certainly not."

"Didn't this Young try to confirm the note with you?"

"He didn't feel it was necessary," Martinetti said. "It was written on my personal stationery, as I said before, and the signature seemed all right to him."

"Did you get the note?"

"Yes. Do you want to see it?"

"If I could."

He took a sheet of bond stationery, folded twice, business-fashion, from the center drawer of the desk and slid it across to me. I unfolded it, read the text—three sentences neatly typed, with no typographical or grammatical errors—and then looked at the signature. It was bold and flowing, with loops instead of dots above the *i*'s.

"How good a forgery is the signature?" I asked Martinetti.

"Good enough to have been taken as mine."

"Do many people have access to papers you've signed? To your personal stationery?"

His lips pulled into a tight, bloodless line, and the irises of his eyes had a peculiar light in them. "Are you intimating that someone I'm acquainted with is responsible?"

"I'm not intimating anything," I said. "I'm only asking some questions. If you'd rather not answer them, that's your prerogative."

The muscles circling his mouth relaxed. "I'm sorry," he said. "I'm on edge; my nerves are rubbed raw."

"You don't have to apologize, Mr. Martinetti."

"Oh Christ," he said wearily, and ran a heavy hand through his hair. "That same damned possibility has occurred to me more than once in the past couple of hours. That someone I know or once knew is connected with this . . . this theft of my son. But I can't conceive of even one person who would do a thing like this."

"How many people now have or have had access to your papers?"

"Quite a few, I suppose. I only keep one girl at my office in Redwood City, for instance, and almost anyone could simply walk in when she's in the rest room or getting coffee from the machine downstairs."

I nodded. There was no purpose in pressing this subject; I could see that it was painful for Martinetti, and I was not supposed to be conducting an investigation or an interrogation anyway. I had to keep reminding myself of my limitations every now and then, because I had been a cop for fifteen years before I went out on my own, and when you've been conditioned to certain methods for that length of time, you find them difficult to break.

I asked, "What did Young tell you about the man?"

"That he was a smooth character, authoritative and well-mannered."

"When you received this call earlier in the afternoon, did he threaten or intimidate you in any way beyond the warning to meet his demands or suffer the consequences?"

"No. He was very amiable, in fact."

"You were unfamiliar with his voice, I take it?"

"Completely."

"Was there anything distinctive about it?"

"How do you mean?"

"Did he have an impediment, an accent, like that?"

"No, it was just an average voice."

"Would you say the caller was educated?"

"I suppose so. His grammar seemed correct."

"Did he let you talk to your son?"

"Just for a moment, yes."

"Was the boy all right?"

"Yes, considering. He was frightened, of course."

I sat back a little, pulling at the lobe of my ear. All of this could have meant something favorable, or it could have meant nothing at all. There are a lot of psychopathic personalities who are adequately educated, and who can be polite and imperative when it behooves them. But I liked it better with that kind of guy than I would have if he had been abusive or obscene, if he had twisted the boy's arm, say, while he was talking on the phone, to let Martinetti know he meant business—that kind of thing.

I got slowly to my feet. "I don't think there's anything else I'll need to know, Mr. Martinetti. If it's all right with you, I'll be down in the morning sometime to wait for the call with you."

"I'd appreciate that, thank you."

I got my wallet from my coat pocket and took out one of the plain white business cards with my home and office telephone numbers embossed on it. I put the card on the desk in front of him, next to the refolded kidnap note. "If anything happens," I said, "or if you want to get in touch with me for any reason, call one of those two numbers. If I go anywhere else, I'll leave word with the answering service that takes care of my office while I'm away."

He nodded, touched the card with one squarely manicured forefinger, and quickly opened the center desk drawer again. He swept the card and the note into it, and extracted a large leather-bound checkbook. "Let me give you a retainer before you go," he said. "Would five hundred dollars be all right for now?"

"Whatever you like," I said.

He wrote quickly with a pen from the marble set, tore the check out, looked at it, and handed it across to me.

I put it in my wallet. We shook hands. Channing was on his feet, too, and I shook hands with him again. He hadn't said a word since his firm disinclination to have anything to do with the ransom drop, and I wondered what kind of things were going around inside that large and ingenious head of his. I did not think I would care for them, whatever they were.

Martinetti motioned to Proxmire, looked at me, and said, "Dean will show you out."

"Fine."

"I'll expect you in the morning, then."

I nodded, watched him sit heavily in the executive's chair and stare with brooding intensity at the glass of liquor on his desk, and then I turned and went over to where Proxmire was waiting by the double-doored entrance.

We went out, and he closed the door. I took a couple of steps along the hall, and he caught my arm lightly and looked at me with eyes that were filled with a liquid fervency. He wanted to say something, but he didn't quite know how to go about it. He bulged his lower lip with his tongue, getting the words arranged. Finally he said, "You'll be very careful, won't you? When you deliver the money? You'll do exactly what you're supposed to do?"

"Did you expect me to start a running gun battle with whoever comes after it?" I said mildly.

He looked a little shocked. "I didn't mean . . . Well, you have a very fine reputation, of course. I just thought that . . . oh God, I don't know what I thought. I'm sorry. Listen, I'm sorry."

"It's all right."

"I'm upset, that's all," Proxmire said. "The boy and I are very close, you see. He's almost like—well, we're very close."

"I understand."

"I don't want anything to happen to him."

"He'll come home okay," I said, putting more assurance in my voice than I felt. "You have to count on that."

"I don't like the idea of paying a ransom," Proxmire said. "We're placing our complete trust in a kidnapper, somebody who preys on *children*, for God's sake! I told Martinetti that the police should be notified. I still think they should."

"It's his son," I said quietly. "And his decision."

"Yes. Yes, I . . . I know."

We went along the hallway and I took my hat off the table, turning toward the door. In that moment I saw the woman standing in the doorway leading to the living room. There were lights on in there now, diffused and amber, and she had a glass in her hand that was half filled with some colorless liquid that might have been water or something considerably stronger. She was leaning against the jamb, as if her legs were too weak to support the full weight of her.

She was maybe thirty, with good breasts and strong hips and the kind of hourglass waist that a big man would have taken pride in spanning with both his hands. Her hair was blond, worn shoulder-length and flipped under at the bottom the way Doris Day used to have hers in those movies with Rock Hudson. Sensuous would be the proper descriptive adjective for her mouth, even void of lipstick as it was at the moment, and tiny dimples attractively centered each of her cheeks. At some other time she might have been almost beautiful, but there was an unhealthy gray pallor to her face now, a glazed, little-girl-lost quality to the azure-blue eyes. She wore a thin paisley-print dress, and her legs and feet were bare.

Proxmire said, "Karyn!" and went to her and touched her shoulder timorously, solicitously. He took the glass out of her hand, looked at it, wet his lips, and carried it a few steps into the living room and put it down on an end table next to a long couch. She made no protest. Her eyes were on me, with a kind of dull comprehension in them.

Proxmire came back and said, "You ought to be in bed, Karyn. The sedative—"

"Oh, damn the sedative," she said dully, and left the doorway and walked unsteadily over to where I stood. She was not drunk; it was pain and fear that caused her shakiness, and the two emotions were alive and volatile inside her.

She stopped a foot away from me, and her tormented eyes roamed my face. "You're the detective Louis called, aren't you?" she asked in a flat, toneless voice.

"Yes, ma'am."

"I'm Karyn Martinetti, Gary's mother."

I did not know what to say to her. I shifted my feet awkwardly, nervously. I had never been any good in a situation like this, facing misery and grief, and that was just one of the dozen or so reasons which had made up my long-range decision to leave the cops. If I could have done it in the least charitably, I would have pushed past her to the door and gotten out of there. I thought: If she starts to cry, I'll do it anyway.

She said, "Will you help us get my son back?"

Proxmire came to my aid then, and I felt better

toward him than I had a few moments earlier. He put his arm tenderly around Karyn Martinetti's shoulders, and she seemed to lean against him as she had leaned against the doorjamb.

Proxmire said, "He's agreed to deliver the ransom money for us, Karyn. He'll come again tomorrow to wait with Louis for the call."

She nodded numbly. "Thank you," she said, and her eyes were still restless on my face.

I had the disquieting, ridiculous feeling that she wanted to kiss my cheek or my hand. I edged toward the door. "I'd better be going now," I said.

"Of course, goodbye," Proxmire said, and his expression added that he knew how I felt. I wondered if he really did. He turned the woman gently away and led her toward the stairs, his head dipped toward her, whispering against her ear. I watched him start her up the stairs, with her moving like an automaton, and then I got the door open and stepped quickly outside.

The air was still warm and sweet and fresh, but it did not make me feel any better.

3

I live in the Pacific Heights district of San Francisco, in what I think is called a Queen Anne Victorian. Old and tired and a bit frowzy, it stands with its turrets and gables proudly erect—like a tycoon's aging mistress with no future and a million glittering memories. It had once been somebody's fine home in the pre-earthquake days of the Barbary Coast and the Chinese tong wars, but time and the scavengers had gotten to it in the thirties and it was subdivided into three fairly large flats. In spite of its age, the location commands a high rent, and if I had not been living there for the past seventeen years under the same owner, I could not have afforded it.

It was almost six-thirty when I turned off Van Ness Avenue onto Clay Street; I had been entangled in the usual rush-hour traffic snarl on the Bayshore, immediately after leaving Hillsborough. There were no parking spaces in the vicinity of my place, not a particularly surprising occurrence, and I had to leave my car a block and a half away. It was considerably cooler in San Francisco than it had been on the Peninsula, and there was a thin, cold wind coming in off the Bay. Fog, in thick gray billows like the smoke from a rubber fire, unfolded across the darkening sky.

I walked quickly, and when I reached the foyer of my building I was winded and conscious of a muted ache in my chest. I tried not to think about that, breathing through my mouth. My mailbox contained two letters, and I put them in my pocket and climbed the dark stairs to the second floor.

The old, faded rose-colored carpet in my apartment was strewn with newspapers and package wrappings and the ashes and butts from an overturned ashtray; the remains of last night's delicatessen supper littered the copper-topped coffee table in front of the sofa. Living alone for a long time does that to you; you get so you don't much care if you come home to neatness or disarray, because mostly you come home alone. I had stopped picking up after myself years ago.

I went over to the thermostat and fussed with it and got some heat coming through the floor furnace. Then I crossed to the curving bay windows and pulled the curtains closed. The fog was heavy now, and I could make out only substanceless shapes in the distance; but on a clear day you could see the sailboats like idyllic toys dotting the silver-blue surface of the Bay, the long and symmetrical contours of the Yacht Harbor, the rising spans of the Golden Gate Bridge and the vast, gentle Pacific beyond.

I took a beer out of the refrigerator in the kitchen and carried it into the living room and sat down to read my mail at the tall mahogany secretary in one corner. One of the letters was a bill from a garage on Mission Street that had done some minor repairs on my car; the other was from a guy in North Carolina, with a new list of pulp magazines he had for sale.

I put the garage bill with some others in one of the pigeonholes. From a lower drawer, I got out the list I had painstakingly typed over a period of several weeks, and compared it with the items outlined in the letter from North Carolina. There were eight issues of *Detective Tales, Star Detective* and *Clues* from the 1930's that I did not have. I sat down and wrote the guy a check and a little note to go with it. When I finished with that, I endorsed Martinetti's check and tucked that into a bank envelope with a deposit slip, and put both envelopes into my coat pocket.

I was not particularly hungry, but I thought I ought to eat something. The refrigerator yielded a package of mortadella and some brick Cheddar cheese, and I made myself two sandwiches on sourdough French bread and ate them standing up at the sideboard. I drank the last of the beer, and then returned to the living room and kicked off my shoes and jacket and pulled down my tie and went to the bookshelves covering the side wall beyond the windows.

The shelves, which I had constructed of metal wall brackets and varying lengths of darkly laminated wood, were the only things in the apartment I made a special effort to keep in order. They contained something more than five thousand copies of detective and adventure pulp magazines dating from the late twenties through the early fifties, when the pulp market collapsed and died.

I had them segregated by title, chronologically, with the quality items like *Black Mask* and *Dime Detective* and *Detective Fiction Weekly* on the upper shelves, and the lesser ones—seventy-five different titles, twenty-two separate Volume One, Number 1—filling the remainder. I had turned some of them around at various points so that their covers faced into the room; they were pretty lurid, most of those covers—salivating fiends in black cloaks or scarlet robes or slouch hats, clutching huge automatics or gleaming daggers; half-nude girls with too-red lips screaming in agony or fear or perhaps even ecstasy—but I liked the effect they gave that staid rose-papered high-ceilinged room. It made the whole setting seem impressionistic, somehow, like a pop-art display.

I had been collecting pulp magazines for twenty-five years, and it was the one consuming passion I had in life. I had grown up on the fringe of the Mission District during the Depression, in a neighborhood not good but not bad, not poor but not well-to-do, and every spare nickel and dime I could cadge or earn went for pulps from the time I was twelve years old. I had stacks of them in the basement storage room of our building, which my mother later gave to the Goodwill without my permission, and I would spend hours in my room or in the basement reading *Black Mask* and the other detective magazines instead of studying.

The pulps fascinated, captivated, me. I couldn't get enough of them. I went to the City College of San Francisco after I graduated high school, and quit after three semesters because the pulps got in the way of my studying and I wouldn't give them up. I went into the Army shortly after that, and until the war broke out I had this soft assignment in Texas as the private chauffeur to a major who was sleeping with half the girls in the nearby town and trying to get next to the other half. I had plenty of time to read, and to plan what I was going to do when I got out of the service; there was a natural fusion of the two after a while, and I knew I was going to go into police work. I had admired the champions of justice that Chandler and Hammett and the other pulp authors wrote about for a long time, and the kind of job they were doing was the kind of job I wanted to do myself.

After Pearl Harbor, I was sent to the South Pacific, and while I was in Hawaii I applied for a position with Military Intelligence. Eventually I passed enough tests to get me into a security unit. I saw no real action, but I learned police work the way the Army teaches it.

I came out late in 1945, after Hiroshima, and when I returned to San Francisco I took the Civil Service exams. In 1946 I went into the Police Academy; I thought I was pretty hot-shot in those days, and I made no secret of the fact that I was both a voracious pulp reader and a self-proclaimed world-beater who was going to set the department on its ear once I got into uniform.

Most of the guys I went through the Academy with thought I was some great fun. They kept pulling gags on me, and calling me "Philip" and "Sam" and "Nick" and "Nero." There was this one in particular, a sort of dour-faced type named Eberhardt, who used to ride me mercilessly, until one day after a drill I took all I was going to take and hit him flush in the mouth. We became good friends after that, the way guys will sometimes after such incidents.

It did not take me long, after I was on the force, to learn that real police work is little more than routine and hard work, pain and suffering, long hours and damned little money, so that you had to fight a constant internal battle to maintain your honesty and your integrity. It was all of those things, and a lot more, but even after I matured and realized and accepted the fact that I wasn't going to set the world on fire, I stuck it out; I stuck it out for fifteen years, because I believed then—and I still believe now—that the prevention of crime and the interests of justice and the law are of vital and immediate concern.

Fifteen years. The last four on the General Works Detail attached to the investigation of homicides. And then one afternoon you answer a squeal to a nice house in the Sunset District, and you walk into a living room that is literally painted with blood—the ceiling, the floors, the walls, the furniture—and sitting there in the middle is a guy with empty eyes cradling a double-edged woodsman's axe, crying, and all around him are what's left of his wife and their two preschool children. You stand there and you look at that, and then you go outside and you puke until there's nothing left, and then you either erect mental defenses to the carnage and step back inside and do the things you have to do as a cop, or you admit that you've had it, you can't take any more, and you get so drunk later that night that you cannot stand without assistance. I was no longer able to erect those mental defenses.

Six months later the State Board of Licenses, after a series of examinations and the posting of a bond, granted me a private investigator's license and I resigned from the force the same day I received the news.

Eberhardt, who is now a Lieutenant of Detectives and who has grown even more dour and cynical over the years, thought I was crazy to have given up fifteen years' seniority toward a pension to open a private agency; he still thinks that, because the agency has been anything but a major success, and he still thinks I'm crazy to keep on reading and collecting pulp magazines. We're good friends in spite of that.

I got down one of the copies of *Black Mask* that I had recently acquired, and hadn't finished reading as yet, and took it over to the sofa. I lit a cigarette, and waited, and when I knew my lungs were going to be all right I opened the magazine and tried to read.

But I could not keep my mind on it. I kept thinking about the Martinetti kidnapping, and the way Karyn Martinetti had looked at me with her eyes full of pain and terror, and the job I had agreed to do. I wished there was some way I could get out of it, now, but I knew that there wasn't; I had committed myself, and unless something radical happened to alter the present status of things, I had to follow through.

I put the magazine down and looked at my watch. Eight o'clock. I wondered if Erika was home, and if she was, what kind of mood she was in. I did not feel much like being alone tonight, but I did not want to have to put up with an argument either.

I kept my telephone in the bedroom, and I walked in there and called her and she answered on the third ring. "Hi, old bear," she said. She sounded pretty chipper. "I suppose you're horny. You never call me otherwise."

I grinned some at that. "I'm more lonely than anything else," I said. "Can I come over and hold your hand?"

"That would be something different, at least."

"Have you got any brandy?"

"Half a bottle."

"Make me a drink," I said. "I'll be there in twenty minutes."

Erika was Erika Coates, and she lived in one of those tasteless stucco-façaded flats on the Marina, near the Presidio. She was a legal secretary with a very proper probate law firm in the financial district; she was thirty-seven years old and twice divorced; she was opinionated and outspoken and somewhat censorious and better in bed than any woman I have ever known.

I met her during the course of a minor investigation I had been conducting for an insurance company two years ago, and asked her out eleven times—four of those in person—before she consented to have so much as an after-work cocktail in Paoli's or the Iron Duke. I had since that time asked her on three separate occasions to marry me, a question I had long past decided I would never be asking any woman, and she had turned me down with gentle regrets each time; she did not want to have to worry about going through a third divorce, she said, but I did not think that was the real reason. The real reason was that she did not like the kind of job I had; it was too unstable for her, I suppose, and the one thing she needed now was stability.

I believe she was in love with me just the same.

I know I was in love with her.

I parked my car in her driveway, as I always did, and went up and rang her bell twice long and twice short in the code we had worked out so that she wouldn't have to come downstairs to see who it was before working the door buzzer. After a couple of seconds the release sounded and I entered and climbed the stairs, and she was waiting for me with her door open and a nice dutiful-wife smile that her eyes said was a fat put-on.

I kissed her, and she was warm and soft in my arms, nuzzling. I stood her away after a time, wondering if the way I felt was mirrored on my face for her to see. Her own face was heart-shaped and puckish, and I thought: Jesus, but she must have been lovely when she was a very young girl. She was still lovely, with this raven-black hair sweeping down like a silken midnight waterfall, glinting metallic-blue highlights in the proper lighting, and wide dancing eyes like fine gray pearls, and a soft quizzical mouth and little gnomelike ears with huge gold gypsy hoops hanging from them. If you looked for them, you could see the tiny age wrinkles that she covered so carefully with skin-toned make-up, the faint cross-hatching effect on the slender column of her throat—but I never looked. She had kept her figure by dieting and exercise, and her breasts were firm and small and her hips lean and her legs ripplingly muscled and sun-lamp brown; tonight she had the package wrapped in a pair of quilted culottes that did nothing for it at all.

She saw me looking at the outfit, and said, "So what did you expect? Something sheer and slinky?"

"Why not?" I said, and patted her, and took her arm and prompted her into the flat.

She had the gas logs burning in the small false fireplace at one end of the room, and it was warm and comfortable in there. The apartment itself was neat and feminine, furnished in Danish Modern, with a lot of frilly throw pillows and some cute white-and-black fluff rugs and a big panda bear sitting in one corner like a naughty child. The walls were filled with wood and glass figurines on dainty shelves, and impressionistic and experimental prints such as Matisse's "Red Studio" and Duchamp's "Nude Descending a Staircase," and a couple of things by Picasso. Over the door leading to the kitchen was a funny little scroll plaque that said: *Evil Is a Very Bad Thing*.

She had the loveseat arranged in front of the fire,

with the bottle of brandy and a silver ice bucket and a couple of glasses on a table beside it. We went over there and sat down, and I mixed a couple of drinks. We sat in silence, our thighs touching. I sipped at my drink, staring at the red-orange glow of the gas fire.

After a time Erika said softly, "What's the matter, old bear?"

"Hmm?"

"You're very contemplative tonight."

"Yeah," I said, "I guess I am."

"What is it?"

"A job, a not very nice job."

"Do you want to talk about it?"

"I don't think so."

"Professional ethics forbid?"

"In this instance, yes."

"Phooey," she said, and there was that faint note of sarcasm and censure in her voice that I did not like to hear, because I knew where it would lead if we allowed it to get out of hand.

I let the remark pass. I got out a cigarette and lit it, and a spell of coughing came on so suddenly that it almost doubled me over on the seat. It seemed loud and consumptive in the quiet apartment. I sat there with the fresh handkerchief over my mouth, listening to the wheezing sounds coming out of my open mouth, not looking at Erika.

And she said very quietly, "When are you going to give up those damned cigarettes, old bear? You smoke three packs every day, or is it four? Your lungs must look like a coal miner's."

"It's not that easy to break the habit—how many times do I have to tell you that?"

"Other people do it every day."

"Well, I'm not other people."

"If you wanted to quit badly enough, you'd find a way."

"Look," I said, "we've been through all this crap before."

"Oh yes, of course we have," she said sardonically. "And that cough keeps getting worse every time I see you. You can't be naïve enough to think there's no connection."

"It's a bronchial thing, that's all."

"Yes? Then why don't you go the doctor for something to clear it up?"

"I don't need to go to a doctor."

"Yes you do, but you won't go anyway. You're afraid of what an examination might reveal. You're afraid a doctor might find cancer or tuberculosis or—"

"Shut up, Erika!" I snapped at her. "Goddamn it, shut up!"

She got to her feet and looked down at me with a pitying expression, and I could feel anger building hot inside me, making the blood pound in my temples. We were coming on another fight, I could sense it; I didn't want it, and yet I knew it was coming and I couldn't find a way to stop it.

"When are you going to grow up?" Erika asked me. "For God's sake, you're forty-seven years old. Do you think you've got the body of a teen-ager? You're susceptible to diseases at your age—"

"Listen," I said, "I don't need any frigging lectures from you!"

I was sorry as soon as I said the words, but it was too late to take them back. Her mouth went small and tight at the corners, and a veil came down like shutters closing over her eyes. "My, haven't we got the pleasant mouth this evening," she said, but all the vitriol was gone from her voice now and there was a kind of controlled and righteous fury in its place.

I said, "Erika . . ."

"Good night," she said. "Please close the door on your way out." And she turned and walked with quick angry strides across the room and through the doorway into the bedroom. The door closed a moment later, loud enough for me to hear, and there was the empty and unmistakably final clicking sound of the key turning in the lock.

I got to my feet and stood there in the now still, suddenly cheerless room for a long time; and then I went over to the front door and slammed out of there, making as much noise as I could.

I drove home in a dark blue funk and made myself a stiff drink that I barely touched and sat listening to the wind tugging at the stripping around the bay windows. After a while the anger drained out of me and left in its wake a deep feeling of depression, of brooding introspection. I went in and got undressed and slipped into the ironposted bed—but I couldn't sleep. I lay there in the dark, wanting a cigarette, not having one.

I kept thinking: She's right. Damn her, she's right.

4

At a few minutes past eight the next morning, tired and stiff-jointed from lack of sleep, I sat staring moodily into a mug of black coffee in the kitchen.

There was a package of Pall Malls beside the mug, and I turned it over and over with the thumb and forefinger of my right hand, not looking at it, trying to make up my mind about them and about the coughing. Cigarettes were a crutch, the satisfaction of a small, obdurate craving, and I was good at telling myself that I could no more give them up than I could give up eating. And yet the thought, strong and vivid now, of what might be growing, festering, in my chest made sweat cold and viscid flow along my body.

I had been putting it out of my mind, effectively blocking it out each time it demanded attention, for better than two months. That's one of the fine things about the human animal: if something bothers you, if something frightens you, you simply put it out of your mind and tell yourself that after a while it will go away of its own accord—and that makes everything okay again. But I could no longer indulge in that kind of speciousness, because the cough was getting worse and because Erika's harsh and acerbic words had brought it all out into the open, into a light I could not flick off.

Well, all right. I had to give up the damned cigarettes, what was the use in kidding myself? I had to quit them cold, none of this tapering-off crap. I could chew toothpicks or gum until the gnawing went away, and after that it would not be so bad at all. Then I would have to go to a doctor and have a chest X-ray, and maybe a thorough physical, to find out about the cough. Maybe what I had told Erika was correct: maybe it was nothing more than a bronchial disorder.

Yeah, and maybe it was cancer.

Jesus, Jesus! I could feel my hands starting to shake, and I swept the package of cigarettes off onto the floor and got up and kicked them behind the stove. I was scared. I had been scared all along.

I thought: What would I do if they told me I had six months to live? What would I say, what would I feel? Or suppose I had to have surgery, to have a lung removed? How would I bear up under that? Because I was petrified of hospitals, of surgical steel, after having been in war-zone hospitals in the South Pacific and having seen things in them no man should ever see. God, maybe it *was* just better to let whatever it was alone, until it either cleared itself up or I just kicked over, but that was not the way it happened, no, an uncle of mine had died of cancer and he had been a hale and hearty man weighing two hundred and fifty pounds all his life and yet he had died at half that weight with his body yellowed and withered and the cancer eating at him, consuming him from within and making him scream with the pain of—

The sudden, strident sound of the telephone bell brought me whirling about. I had taken the phone on its long cord into the kitchen and put it down on the sideboard earlier, with the idea of calling Erika, but I hadn't been able to do it; I had forgotten the thing was there.

I took a couple of deep breaths, getting the dark thoughts out of my mind, getting calm, and then I went over and answered it on the third ring. It was a secretary to Allan Channing, crisp and efficient and precise. She wanted to know if it would be possible for me to come by his office in San Mateo before I attended to my other commitment on the Peninsula. I said it would, and wondered what Channing wanted of me; but I did not ask. The secretary would not have known anyway.

I hung up and went back and stared at the coffee some more. I was not looking forward to what lay ahead on this day, or at any time in the near future, and suddenly I wished I were on a boat somewhere—an old bugeye sloop, perhaps, clean and sleek and well-provisioned—alone on that boat with the song of the sea wind in my ears and the feel of salt spray on my face. But that was a never-never land, a peace and a serenity I could never aspire to because I was too practical, too tightly bound to the city and her chaotic ways. I knew that, and the knowledge saddened me. I had today, and maybe tomorrow, and maybe a lot of tomorrows—but I had cold stark reality, too, and I could never escape from it . . .

I shook myself and thought: Come down a little, will you? Christ! I got a box of wooden toothpicks out of one of the cupboards and took that and the telephone into the bedroom. I slipped the toothpicks into the pocket of my suitcoat, and put the coat on, and found a tie that looked all right against the pale yellow of the only clean shirt I had in from the laundry. I stared at the telephone for a few seconds, but I still could not bring myself to call Erika; later, tomorrow, after I was finished with this Martinetti business, after I had made an appointment with a doctor. Tomorrow.

The same commuter traffic I had gotten caught in the night before, in reverse, tangled the Bayshore, and it took me forty minutes to travel the twenty miles to San Mateo. The fog was thick and gray and cold as far south as Millbrae, and then the sky cleared and it was warm and balmy again, a nice autumn morning that I could not enjoy at all.

I stopped at a Standard station for gas, and asked directions to the address Allan Channing's secretary had given me on the phone. The attendant told me how to get to it.

The building turned out to be a sprawling, ranch-style complex with a covered gallery bisecting it into two wings, and a solid rear section. There was a big lacquered redwood sign hung between two gnarled posts next to the entrance drive; the words *San Mateo Professional Center* were neatly wood-burned across the top, and below them were wide strips of brass lettered in white in two rows of six each. I saw that the building's offices were occupied by several doctors and dentists, a certified public accountant, a lawyer; Channing's name, with the words *Financial Consultant* below it, was next to the bottom on the right-hand row—Number 9.

I parked my car in the diagonally striped lot to one side and walked around to the gallery. The various offices opened off of that, and it was cool and aromatic in there; multishaped wooden planters set into the stone floor were filled with trimmed cypress and laurel and red-and-white fuchsia and a half-dozen other plants and flowers. The center portion of the rear wall was comprised of a rough-stone waterfall-and-fountain, with pieces of colored tile forming a square mosaic pond for the water trickling down from a mossy, cavelike opening in the rock. Channing's office was next to that, on the right; a plaque identical to the one on the sign by the drive—a little larger—was fitted to the door at eye level. I turned the knob and went inside.

I stood in a reception room like a hundred other reception rooms: thick saffron-colored rug on the floor, inoffensive outdoor prints on the walls, a settee and three chairs made of walnut and fitted with tweed cushions, three end tables and a low glass-topped table in front of the settee, with copies of *Time* and *Newsweek* and *Fortune* and the *Wall Street Journal* neatly arranged on it, and a small functional metal desk occupying one corner.

Behind the desk, fingers flying over the keys of a small typewriter, was a thin, angular henna-haired woman in her mid-forties, wearing a mannish gray suit and a couple of ounces of lavender perfume. She had pinched cheeks and hazel eyes that looked as if they had seldom, if ever, shone with the heat of passion. Channing was apparently a no-nonsense boy when it came to business.

The woman finished what she was typing, let the automatic return flip the carriage back, and looked up at me with professional aloofness. Her smile was as manufactured as the color of her hair. "Yes, may I help you?"

I gave her my name, and said that Mr. Channing was expecting me. She nodded crisply and went primly through one of the two doors to the right of her desk, both of which were marked *Private*. I stood on the thick carpet with my hat in my hands, waiting. I tried not to think how badly I wanted a cigarette. A minute or so passed, and then the secretary came out and held the door and told me I could go in.

It was by no means a sumptuous office; it was a place where the sober task of making money was performed, and that told me a little more about what kind of man Allan Channing was.

He was standing by the windows that comprised the upper half of the wall behind his desk, wearing an olive-green tailor-made suit and a white shirt with French cuffs and gold links with a black onyx "C" on each of them. Sunlight slanted in through Venetian blinds partially closed over the windows, casting thinly pale bars across his face, and I could see deep purplish circles beneath the innocent eyes. He looked as if he had not slept very much the night before.

He came away from the windows as I entered, and we shook hands. He asked gravely how I was, indicated one of the two visitors' chairs, and then went behind the desk and sank wearily into his swivel chair. He pressed the balls of his thumbs against his closed eyelids, held them there for a time, sighed, and looked up and across at me.

"The reason I asked you to stop by," he said, "is a more or less confidential one. I'd appreciate it if whatever is said here this morning goes no further."

"All right."

"Thank you." He got his lower lip between his teeth and worried it, as if he was not quite sure how to begin. Then, abruptly, he said, "I'd like your opinion."

"On what, Mr. Channing?"

"This thing with Lou's son. You seem to know about these matters."

"Not much," I said.

"Well," Channing said. He rubbed the back of his neck. "What I'd like to know—what usually happens? I mean, after the ransom money is paid, is the victim usually allowed to go free?"

I frowned slightly. "There's no way of predicting that," I told him. "It takes a certain kind of person to carry off a kidnapping, and you never know in advance what he's going to do."

"Would you say the chances were likely?"

"I wouldn't say."

"Yes, but there must be statistics . . ."

"Statistics don't mean anything at all in an individual kidnapping," I said. "Any police officer would tell you that."

"You think Lou should have called the police, don't you? Instead of flatly agreeing to pay the ransom."

"Yes, I do."

"But you didn't try to convince him of that yesterday."

"No, and not because it would have negated my fee if I'd been successful, either."

"I didn't mean to intimate that," Channing said quickly.

"Martinetti's mind was made up, and no amount of talking I could have done would have convinced him otherwise. Besides, it wasn't and isn't my place. This involves *his* son, not mine or anyone else's, and he's got the right to make whatever decision he thinks is best."

"Of course, of course."

I watched him take a cellophane-wrapped Havana Partagás cigar from a walnut-and-bronze humidor on his desk; he had some connections, all right, to have gotten a brand like that into this country. He unwrapped it slowly, and used a silver trimmer from his desk to snip off the end. He rolled the cigar around in his fingers, and looked at me again. "What are the odds on the police catching the kidnapper?" he asked. "After the ransom is paid?"

Christ, what was the point of all this? My nerves were frayed this morning, and his bandying about was not helping matters any. He had something on his mind, but he was taking a hell of a long time putting voice to it.

I said, "Sometimes they catch them, and sometimes they don't. It depends to a large degree on circumstance. Again, it's not something you can predict."

"I see," Channing said. He used a bronze lighter on the cigar, rolling it in studied half-turns through the flame. The smoke was fragrant and whitish-gray, and I watched it with a kind of hunger. My hands were tight on my knees.

Channing leaned back in the chair and looked at the cigar, and his guileless eyes were troubled. He said, "I . . . suppose I should be frank with you."

"That would be nice."

"I'm in an uncomfortable position," he said slowly. "I have always been a very cautious man when it came to money, you see. That is how I managed to attain the position of wealth and stability which I command today."

I waited, not speaking.

"Lou Martinetti isn't like that. He takes gambles, foolish gambles. In the past few months he has made some

44

extremely ill-advised investments, and consequently has lost a considerable amount of money."

I kept on waiting.

"Last night he and I made a careful check of his negotiable assets," Channing said. "He doesn't have three hundred thousand dollars. He couldn't begin to raise even half that much, not in one week or one month. To put it simply, Lou Martinetti is not too far removed from bankruptcy."

I had not expected that, but I was not as surprised as I might have been; the kind of businessman Martinetti had a reputation of being, the state of his finances at various times in the past, made such a revelation something less than startling. But I thought I saw the motivation for Channing's earlier questions; the point of all this was becoming very clear.

I said, "He's asked you for the ransom money, is that it?"

Channing was silent for a long moment, a faintly pained expression at the corners of his mouth. Then, slowly, he nodded. "Yes. A loan. I'm not in the habit of loaning money, not even to personal friends, not for any reason. And three hundred thousand dollars is quite a lot of money."

I agreed that it was.

"But on the other hand, if the ransom isn't paid and Gary is . . ." He couldn't bring himself to say the words. "If that were to happen, it would be on my conscience, do you see? I couldn't bear a cross like that."

"Are you going to give him the money?"

"I don't really have a choice, do I?"

"Apparently not."

"I suppose, when I asked you here today, I just wanted some reassurance that everything was going to work out—that Gary would be returned safely after the ransom payment, and that I would get my money back. Not that Martinetti wouldn't repay it; he would, certainly, as soon as he was able. But that might possibly be a period of years."

I said, without thinking, "And you wouldn't like to have three hundred thousand dollars of your money not producing any returns."

Channing looked at me sharply for a brief instant, and then he sighed audibly and carefully tapped the ash off the end of his cigar into a bronze ashtray. "I'm not a hard man," he said, and there was a note of defensiveness in his voice. "Oh, I've stepped on a few people in my life; what successful man hasn't? But I'm not a driving force, the way Martinetti is."

"That's your concern, Mr. Channing," I said. I did not want to listen to any rationalizations this morning.

"Yes," he said, "I suppose it is."

I got on my feet. "If there's nothing more, I've got to be on my way."

"No, nothing more," he said. He stood, too, and extended his hand. I took it. "Are you going to Lou's now?"

"Yes."

"I'll be there later this afternoon. It will take some time to gather the money together from various banks."

I said I would see him later, and let myself out. I went quickly to where I had left my car, and got a toothpick from my coat pocket and chewed on it. I thought:

Jesus, it must be hell to live with yourself if you're a man like that.

I started the car and swung down onto El Camino Real and turned north there, toward Hillsborough.

5

Martinetti was sitting alone on the terrace, at a wrought-iron table under a huge fringed umbrella. I could see him as I came up the path from the front gate, but instead of cutting across the lawn on the circular stepping stones leading to the terrace from an opening in the low retaining wall, I went peremptorily to the front door and rang the bell.

The thin dark-haired maid—Cassy—let me in and put my hat on the same hall table and escorted me wordlessly through the huge living room and through a sliding glass door at the left of the bay window. I did not see any sign of Karyn Martinetti or Proxmire, the secretary. The living room was dark and silent.

There was a white cloth spread over the table at which Martinetti sat, and on it was a silver coffee service and a crystal decanter of what looked like brandy. The cup in front of him was half full, and his face was flushed lightly. The gray eyes were sunken in discolored pouches, and had a haunted look to them; no magnetism on this day.

He turned the haunted eyes on me as I came out onto the terrace and put his chin down a half-point in greeting. I sat in the chair on his right. He said, hollowly, to the maid, "Bring another cup, would you please, Cassy?"

"Yes, sir," she said, and went away.

We sat there in silence for a time, looking out over the rippling blue-green water in the pool, to the drive and a high green bordering hedge beyond it. It was warm and quiet, and you could hear sparrows and fat-breasted robins chattering in the trees. I wanted a cigarette so badly that the thought of one made saliva flow hotly in my mouth.

I said finally, "No word yet, Mr. Martinetti?" but it was a rhetorical question. I could tell just by looking at him that there had been none.

He shook his head and put the coffee cup to his mouth and drank deeply from it with his eyes closed. A shudder passed through him, brief and violent, and then he put the cup down very carefully with hands that were steady only by an effort of will.

The maid came back with a china cup on a small silver tray and put the cup down in front of me and poured coffee from the silver service. Then she refilled Martinetti's cup and went away again. I watched him add a couple of fingers from the decanter, and poured milk and stirred sugar into my own coffee.

I said quietly, "You ought to get some sleep, Mr. Martinetti. I can watch the phone for you."

"No, I'm all right," he said. "I'm fine."

"Whatever you say."

He drank from his cup again. I hoped he would

not get drunk; in this sort of situation the clearer the thinking the better off everything was going to be. But he looked as if he could handle the liquor well enough, and I thought better of saying anything to him about it. If Gary Martinetti had been my son, maybe I would have felt like getting a little tight, too.

There was not much we could say to one another, and we sat and listened to the morning sounds. I drank coffee and chewed toothpicks and tried not to think about anything at all. An hour passed, and I knew I was not going to make it. My nerves were like the sparking ends of live wires. I kept telling myself to remember the cough, to remember my uncle who had died wasted of cancer, but I wasn't coughing now and my lungs felt fine and it just wasn't any goddamned use, not with the tension building inexorably with each passing second.

I excused myself and went along the lawn to the path and out to where I had left my car. In the glove compartment I found three packages of cigarettes that I had known were there all along. I got one of them out and tore it open and shook out a cylinder and lit it and breathed in the smoke like it was ambrosia. I closed my eyes and leaned against the side of the car, and there was a weak feeling of completion in the pit of my stomach, the kind of feeling you have after a sexual orgasm. I was not coughing, and the barrier was back up in my mind; I could not even tell myself what a weak damned fool I was.

I put the opened package and another one in my coat pocket and walked back across the footbridge, through the gate. As I approached the terrace, I saw that Karyn Martinetti had come out and was sitting next to her husband at the table. She still had that little-girl-lost expression in her eyes, but there was some color in her cheeks and she'd put on a touch of coral lipstick. The blond hair was pulled back severely into a ponytail and tied with a black velvet ribbon, and she was dressed in a thin white sweater and a wrap-around skirt and white tennis shoes.

She tried a smile for me as I sat down, but it was weak and painful for her and she put it away almost immediately.

I said, "Good morning, Mrs. Martinetti. How are you feeling?"

"Oh, lovely," she answered in a dull voice. "I can't remember when I've ever felt as lovely as I do at this very moment."

"Karyn, for God's sake!" Martinetti snapped at her.

She brought her arms up and hugged herself as if she was suddenly chilled. "I'm sorry," she said very softly. "I'm sorry."

"Why don't you go upstairs and lie down?" Martinetti said. "You aren't helping us or yourself being down here."

"I don't want to be alone, Lou."

"Cassy will stay with you."

"I want to stay here."

He moistened his lips. "All right, then."

And the three of us sat, waiting. The sun climbed perpendicular in the pale blue autumn sky, and then started its slow and repetitive descent toward the western horizon. Cassy came out with a plate of sandwiches and some chilled raw vegetables, but none of us seemed to be very hungry. I smoked three more cigarettes, carefully, like a junior high school kid locked in the bathroom, and nothing happened in my chest. The tension was still strong in the air, growing stronger, but I could handle it now; I had my crutch back.

Shortly past one the silver MG roadster I had seen the day before pulled across the wooden bridge into the drive and Dean Proxmire got out. He came hurrying across the lawn and onto the terrace, harried and pale and somber. His eyes, when they touched Karyn Martinetti's face, held a deep concern—and something else that I could not quite read.

Martinetti said, "Did you take care of things at the office?"

"Yes. Any news yet?"

"Nothing."

"Christ, what's taking him so long?"

"I wish to God I knew."

Proxmire sank into the fourth chair at the table, looked at Karyn Martinetti again, looked at the back of his hands. He said softly, bitterly, "The bastard. The lousy bastard."

More silence. Five minutes passed. And then, suddenly, Martinetti scraped his chair back and got to his feet. He lifted the near-empty decanter off the table. "I'm going into the study," he said. He looked at me. "Are you coming?"

I said, "All right," and stood up.

"Dean?"

"If you don't mind, I'll stay here with Karyn," Proxmire said.

"Why should I mind?" Martinetti said.

They looked at one another steadily, and something indefinable passed between them. I wondered what kind of relationships lay below the proper surface in this nice Hillsborough house—but it wasn't any of my business. I had enough to worry about.

Martinetti turned on his heel and I followed him through the living room and down the side hallway and through the ornate double doors into his study. He went over to the bar and got a glass from behind it and took that and the decanter to his desk. I sat on the couch facing him. He said, "Help yourself if you want a drink," and poured his glass three-quarters full.

The silence deepened after a time, seeming to gain volume, so that it was like a screaming cacophony of sound just beyond the range of hearing. I developed a headache from listening to it, from the tension of waiting. I made a couple of attempts at conversation, but Martinetti was not having any. He sat there drinking and staring at a point high on the wall above his stereo components, moving just a little every now and then to ease a cramped muscle. He did not look at me at all.

I got up a couple of times and prowled the room, looking at the books on the shelves, the hammered-copper curios, the stereo unit. The books were stuffy English classics and modern romances and biographical studies, the records were fugues, Chopin and Bartok and Shostakovich, mood and dinner music—but no jazz; none of it much interested me. I went through a half-dozen more cigarettes, and there was a rasping in my chest now and I knew that the next one would bring on the coughing. I could hear Erika's voice saying over and over in my mind, *When are you going to grow up? Do you think you've got the body of a teen-ager? When are you going to grow up?*

The call came at nine minutes past four.

The sound of the bell seemed to explode in the strained, deafening hush of the room. Martinetti came half out of his chair in a convulsive movement, freezing there, his eyes bulging toward the phone, his hands gripping the edge of the desk. I got on my feet and swallowed against a dryness in my throat.

Martinetti gave a kind of shiver, as if to regenerate mobility, and then caught up the receiver with his right hand. He said, "Hello?" in a hoarse whispering voice.

He did not say anything else for more than a minute. He held the instrument pressed tightly to his ear, the hand white and rigid around it, his face a mask of intense concentration as he listened. Finally he said, "Yes, I understand," paused, said, "Please, I'm doing just as you want, don't hurt my—"

His mouth clamped shut, and the hand holding the receiver dropped slowly to his side. After a moment he reached out and placed the handset in its cradle and sank back down in his chair. He put his head in his hands.

I went up to the desk and saw that his shoulders were trembling almost imperceptibly, as if he might be silently weeping. I gave him thirty seconds, and then I said softly, "Mr. Martinetti."

His head jerked up, and he looked at me as if he were seeing me for the first time. There was a grayness to the taut skin across his cheekbones, but his eyes were dry.

"Is anything wrong?" I asked him. "The call—?"

"No, no," he said, and took a deep shuddering breath. "I . . . it's just that I . . . I feel drained, purged, after all that waiting. Do you understand?"

"Yes," I said.

There was a sharp rapping on the entrance doors, and one of them swung open and Proxmire came quickly into the study. Karyn Martinetti was behind him, her face the color of dirty snow. Proxmire said, "We heard the telephone. Was that—?"

Martinetti said, "Yes."

"What did he say? Is Gary all right?"

"He's all right."

"Well, what did he *say?*"

Martinetti looked at him dully.

"Damn it, man, did he give you instructions for delivering the ransom money?" Proxmire demanded.

Martinetti seemed not to notice. "Yes."

I said, "When will it be?"

"Tonight."

"What time?"

"Ten o'clock."

"Where?"

"There's a dirt road leading off Old Southbridge Road, up in the hills back of San Bruno," Martinetti said woodenly. "You're to drive in there exactly one mile. You'll leave your car in a turnaround there and walk down the embankment at the left side of the road until you reach a flat sandstone rock. You'll put the money on top of the rock and return to your car. Then you'll turn the car around and go back the way you came."

I thought it over. "It sounds kind of isolated. He'd be leaving himself wide open to a trap, if you'd played it the other way and called the police."

"Not really," Proxmire said. "I know that area, and there's another road at the bottom of the embankment. If he waits down there, there are a dozen streets he can slip into once he has the money."

I nodded, and said to Martinetti, "Was there anything else?"

"A warning," he answered softly. "No police, and no tricks. If he's picked up, and doesn't return to a certain place at a certain time, there is someone with the boy who has instructions to . . ." He broke off, and dry-washed his face savagely with both hands. "When he has the money, we'll get a call telling us where to find Gary. That's all."

I took a breath. "Have you got a map of the drop area?"

"I think there's one in the hall table."

"I'll get it," Proxmire said. He went to where Karyn Martinetti was standing with both hands hooked onto the couch in front of the fireplace, took her arm, and led her out of the room.

Martinetti got up and took the decanter over to the alcove. He poured a small one into his glass, drank it off, shuddered, and put the decanter away behind the bar. He said, "I've had enough of that."

I did not say anything, but I thought that he was probably right.

Proxmire came back alone, with a map of the San Francisco Peninsula. I spread it open on Martinetti's desk. He pointed out the area, and the spot of the drop as near as he could tell it by scale. I familiarized myself with it, and with the route I would take to get there, and then folded the map and put it into my coat pocket.

It was about the kind of thing I had expected: simple enough, well planned, not much margin for error. Except for a few minutes alone in the darkness with three hundred thousand dollars, it would be a cakewalk for me; as long as nothing went wrong, it did not seem to be worth anywhere near the fifteen hundred dollars I was getting for it.

6

Time crawled like a fat gray slug.

Seconds became lifetimes, and minutes became miniature eternities. The waiting before had been bad, but this was something else again. You could feel the pressure building, building, like a tangible entity through the dark and silent house.

Martinetti had professed a desire to be alone, and Proxmire and I had gone out to sit in the living room with Karyn Martinetti. It was a nice living room—a copper-hooded fireplace similar in styling but somewhat larger than the one in the study, some good stark seascapes of the cypress-dotted coastline between Monterey and Big Sur, a low rock planter wall that right-angled into the room between the bay window and the fireplace and had some green vines twisting down along the stones almost to the floor—but the air in there seemed stagnant, as if it had been closed up for a very long time. I had to breathe through my mouth after a while. My headache gained magnitude to where the dull pain had a lancing rhythm, like the muted throb of a two-cycle engine.

Cassy came with coffee and more sandwiches. I got two cups of the strong black liquid down, but the ham-on-whole-wheat seemed to stick in a glutinous mass in my throat. Proxmire and Karyn Martinetti neither ate nor drank anything; they were sitting on the couch, at opposite ends, like two sculpted bookends holding up nothing at all.

The door chimes sounded just past six, and Proxmire was on his feet and moving with long strides into the entrance hall before the echo of them faded into silence. From where I was sitting I could look into the hall, and I saw him open the door and admit Allan Channing.

Channing, dressed as he had been that morning, was carrying a brown leather suitcase in his right hand. It looked very heavy. He glanced into the living room and saw me, but he made no acknowledgment. He told Proxmire that Martinetti was waiting for him, and the two of them disappeared into the side hall.

A couple of minutes passed, and Proxmire came back and sat down stoically and watched Karyn Martinetti out of half-lidded eyes. I tried another cigarette, and the coughing started, and I ground it out immediately. My chest felt as if a steel band were being tightened around it, suffocating me. The weight of this whole thing was beginning to settle squarely on my shoulders now; the others were assuming passive roles. If anything went wrong tonight . . .

Well, all right, I told myself. All you have to do is follow the instructions. No games and no heroics; hell, you're not even inclined that way. That's simple enough, isn't it?

I decided I needed some fresh air. I went out onto the terrace and walked over to the outdoor bar. It was constructed of stone, with a slant-backed wooden roof; four leather-topped stools were arranged before it. I sat on one of them, facing toward the house and pool.

It was full dark now, and the night air held the clean, mild bite of autumn frost. The stars seemed cold and synthetic in the ebon sky. There was a yellow-gold half moon, like a canted, halved orange slice, sitting directly overhead; the edges of its curvature were of a slightly darker coloration, rindlike. It shone on the water in the swimming pool in a long, slender, golden streamer.

I felt better, sitting out there. The drapes were pulled closed over the bay window, and I could not see inside; I thought that was just as well. From the direction of the creek running across the rear of the Martinetti property, there was the commingled sound of crickets and night birds singing full-throated and yet very soft, without worry and without sadness.

The music they made seemed to have a deep lure for me, like that haunting oboe melody in Hamlin town, and I left the outdoor bar and walked to the creek across the thick dew-scented grass. I reached the bank and the heavy shadows cast by the tall, staid eucalyptus, and began to walk toward the rock garden at the far end of the grounds.

The creek bed was rocky and littered with branches and leaves and silt. A thin, tired stream meandered across the stones in the exact center, but when the winter rains came, the creek would be swollen and rushing with muddy brown run-off water. The banks were irregular and not at all steep, and I thought to hell with it and climbed down to give the frail and weary stream some company for a short while.

I walked slowly, listening to the night music, smelling the dampness of the earth and of green things growing fresh and strong. The cold air felt very good in my lungs, and I took long swallows of it and thought about nothing at all.

I drew parallel with the rock garden, and the stunted shapes of the shrubs and plants were silky black shadows against the lighter color of the sky. I reached the high redwood boundary fence and went past it fifteen yards or so, and there was a shelf at the bole of one of the slender eucalyptus covered with dry leaves and dark green Spanish moss. I sat down on that, in the deep shadow of the tree, and looked into the darkness beyond the opposite bank, where thick undergrowth obliterated the rear grounds of another home. The orange-slice moon was visible between the branches of the trees overhead.

I had been there about five minutes, sitting motionless on the natural bank chair, when I heard the sound of footfalls shuffling through the foliage at the base of the redwood fence, coming around it. There was silence for the space of several heartbeats, and then voices, clear and distinct, came drifting to me on the scented night air.

"Oh God, Dean, hold me, just hold me!"

"Easy, honey, easy now."

"I just couldn't stand it another minute in there!"

"I know, I know."

Proxmire and Karyn Martinetti. I turned my head without moving my body, and I could see them standing back against the fence, two dark forms blended together, embracing. I held my breath, listening, not wanting to listen at all.

Several seconds passed before they parted, but they remained standing very close together. Karyn Martinetti's voice said fervently, "Dean, tell me everything is going to be all right. Tell me Gary will come home safely."

"He will, honey, he *will*."

"I'm so afraid!"

"Don't let yourself be."

"If . . . if anything happens to him, I don't know what I'll do!"

"Shh, now, nothing is going to happen to him."

"I wish I could believe that!"

"You can believe it, you have to believe it."

"God, oh God, why did this nightmare have to happen? Everything seemed to be perfect for us, you and Gary and me. I could have left Lou just as we planned, and gone to Massillon to my parents and let a lawyer handle the whole matter . . ."

"It can still work out that way."

"No, no, don't you see? I always thought Lou was indifferent where Gary was concerned, that he didn't really care about him at all. But I was wrong, Dean, because he's about to pay three hundred thousand dollars to get him back. I didn't think he would, but I thank the Lord that he is, and I can't hate him any more."

"No, you can't hate him, but you can't go on living with him either, Karyn."

"I know that. But he won't just let me leave with Gary now. He'll fight me for custody, if only because he's made an investment and he hates to lose on any kind of investment. That's the way he is, Dean, I know!"

"If he wants a court battle, we'll give him one."

"Suppose he charges me with adultery?"

"He can't prove anything."

"But he *knows*. Isn't that enough?"

"In a court of law, no."

"The scandal would be sufficient to give him custody of Gary, and I couldn't bear that!"

"Not if we fought it long and hard enough."

"We don't have the money for that kind of battle."

"There are ways of getting money."

"How?"

"You let me worry about that."

The shadows blended together again.

"Oh, darling, I love you so very much!"

Soft, liquid sounds—the sounds of a woman weeping. I felt suddenly very cold, sitting there, embarrassed for them and more embarrassed for myself. There could not have been a worse time for me to overhear a conversation like that; it made this whole damned affair that much more painful, my own position that much more awkward. I felt a little sorry for Martinetti, but I felt a whole lot sorrier for his son.

The shapes divided again, after a couple of minutes, and Proxmire's voice said, "We'd better be getting back, honey, before we're missed. Are you all right now?"

"Yes."

"Everything will work out, believe me. Try to be brave."

"I'll try."

I listened to their footfalls moving away, not watching them, not moving. I gave them five minutes to get back inside the house, and then I got up slowly and walked back along the creek bed to a spot opposite the outdoor bar. I climbed up the bank and went across the grass and onto the terrace and inside through the sliding glass door at the side of the bay window.

There was no one in the living room; maybe she'd gone upstairs to lie down, and he'd gone with her. It was just as well, because I did not want to have to look at either of them. I sat down on the couch and poured some cold coffee into my cup and balanced the saucer on my knee. My wristwatch said that it was a quarter past seven. I had two hours yet; it was going to be more like two days. I wanted nothing so much as I wanted to be finished with this whole thing.

A half-hour went by, dragging chains. I got up finally and stepped to where a console color television sat at an angle against the near wall, and turned it on just to have some sound, some movement. When Proxmire put in an appearance ten minutes later, I was watching a guy in an astronaut suit exhibit the patience of Job with a five-year-old kid who kept demanding another cartoon.

He looked at me as if I were committing an unnatural sin. "For Christ's sake, do you have to have that thing on *now?*"

"Would you rather I locked myself in the coat closet until it's time to leave?"

"Listen, you don't have to get snotty."

"No," I said, "I guess I don't."

"We're all on edge around here, you know," he said, and went over on the other side of the planter wall and stared at the empty fireplace.

Another half-hour crawled away, and then it was eight-thirty. I lit a cigarette and coughed my way through it and went outside again for more air. I walked around. I sat by the pool. I came back into the living room and sat on the couch some more. Nine o'clock.

I gave it another five minutes; then I went out through the entrance hall and down the side hallway and knocked on the study doors. Martinetti's voice said to come in, and I opened one of the doors and walked inside.

Martinetti was standing at the bar, but not drinking, and Channing was sitting on the couch; they looked like a couple of old, old men in the pale light from the lamp on the desk—perhaps for different reasons. The suitcase was on the desk, too.

I said, "I think it's about time I was going."

Martinetti nodded and rubbed wearily at his haunted eyes. "I was going to give you another ten minutes, but maybe it's better if you leave a little early."

"Maybe so." I had trouble meeting his gaze, after what I had overheard by the creek.

"You know exactly what you are supposed to do?"

I said I knew.

He nodded again. "I'm very grateful to you," he said. "For being here today and for doing this tonight."

"Sure," I said.

Martinetti took the suitcase off the desk and started toward the door. Channing got to his feet wordlessly, and we followed Martinetti out into the entrance hall. Proxmire was there, and when we stepped outside he came tagging along. We looked like a single file of grim-visaged bank examiners walking along the gravel path and through the gate and across the footbridge.

There was a street lamp about ten feet in back of my car, and it cast a pool of pale amber light on the dark, silent street. I got inside the car, and Martinetti handed me the case and I put it on the seat beside me.

He said, "Luck."

I tried a little smile, and nodded, and made a sign

with my thumb and forefinger. He stepped back and I got the car going.

When I reached the corner, I looked up at my rear-view mirror. They were all standing there on the edge of the amber pool of light, three black silhouettes against the illumination, watching me. Then I turned the corner and they were gone, and I was alone.

7

I drove out of Hillsborough and onto El Camino Real, north. I drove slowly, both hands on the wheel, concentrating on the pavement sweeping by beneath the car's headlights and letting the rest of my mind lie fallow.

Traffic was heavy, as it has a tendency to be in the evenings, through Burlingame and Millbrae; when I reached San Bruno, it thinned out considerably and I could make a little better time. At Sneath Lane, I turned left and followed it past the Golden Gate National Cemetery and across Junipero Serra Boulevard, and then across Skyline, and finally into the hills well south of Riverside Park.

Skyline seemed to be the dividing line between a bright, cold, clear sky and the restless tendrils of blanketing fog that drifted in above Pacifica from the ocean. The fog was thick and wet in the hills, and gave an eerie, disembodied quality to the lights of the Peninsula behind and below me. I put on my windshield wipers after a while and closed the wing window; the wind was sharp and icy up there, and the penetrating dampness of the sea mist had sucked away all the warmth inside the car in a matter of a few seconds. I switched the heater on to the *High* position. Thick, stale air rushed through the floor and dash vents, but it seemed still to be cold, as if the moistness had somehow gotten permanently into the upholstery and the headliner.

I found Old Southbridge Road without difficulty, and the narrow dirt road leading off it. I slowed there, just as I made the turn, and pulled off to the side and stared down as much of the road as I could see in the swirling, enveloping grayness. There were trees scattered on both sides—oak and bay and eucalyptus—and they had a strange, ethereal quality, like nightmarish illustrations in a book by Poe. There were not many homes in this particular area, and consequently, few lights and scarcely any sound at all except for the faint, wet slithering of the fog through the branches of the trees.

I looked at my watch, and it was ten minutes to ten. Okay. I checked the odometer, and then pulled out onto the road again and drove along exactly one mile. The fog swallowed the road behind me, and seemed to part reluctantly under the probing yellow cones of my headlight beams. The turnaround was there, on my right, a flat space beneath several bunched eucalyptus with their bark peeling off in great gray strips like dead and diseased skin. I stopped the car there and shut off the engine and the headlamps.

It was heavy dark, and I could just see the outlines of the trees on the opposite side of the road. What night sounds there were seemed muted and directionless, distorted by the thick and enshrouding fog. The luminescent dial of my wristwatch showed that it was now five minutes to ten.

I lit a cigarette, and in the flare of the match I could see my face reflected back at me in the door window; it looked pinched and apprehensive, a little old, a little tired. I shook out the match and dragged slowly on the cigarette and tried to ignore the viscid coldness which seemed to have settled between my shoulder blades.

Three minutes to ten.

I stabbed out the cigarette in the ashtray and caught up the suitcase in my right hand. All right, I thought. Here we go. I stepped out of the car and shut the door without slamming it. Cold tongues of fog licked at my face, wet and feathery, and I shivered involuntarily and hunched my shoulders inside the suit jacket. I wished I had had the sense to bring an overcoat; it was going to take me a long time to get warm again on this night.

I crossed the wet, dark, empty road and stood on the embankment at the opposite side. I could just make out the slope of the bank dropping away gently between a bay and an oak, the formless and unidentifiable shadows of undergrowth—but that was all. I could not see the road below; the mist was an impenetrable pocket, and as thick and clinging and grayly vibratory as gelatin.

If he's down there, I thought, he can't see me either. But he knows I'm here. He'd have heard the car.

I took a firmer grip on the suitcase, hefting it in my hand, and started down the embankment. The footing was none too good—the ground had a soft, spongelike consistency, strewn with wet leaves and moss, and I was forced to pick my way a half-step at a time, with my left arm flung out for balance and my right holding the case in close to my body. I had visions of getting lost, of not being able to find that flat sandstone rock, of missing the ten o'clock deadline, so that the kidnapper became frightened by the delay and panicked and ran. But that kind of thoughts were not getting me anything but uptight; I put them out of my mind and kept working my way down the slope.

Moments passed and it did not seem as if I had gone more than five or six feet, but when I turned to look upward, I could no longer see the top of the embankment. Visibility was maybe two feet in each direction. I took another step forward and down, careful, another, another— and then the rock was there, looming up out of the sodden turf like an oval picnic table, smooth and flat and shiny with mist.

I let breath out between my teeth in a soft, sibilant sigh and went carefully to the rock and put the suitcase down on top of it. As I straightened up, there was the sound of a twig cracking, a thin report, from somewhere below and to my right. I worked saliva into my mouth and turned and started up the embankment toward the road, leaning forward with my hands low to the ground in case I lost my footing.

I was almost to the roadbed again when I heard the scream.

It was a man's voice, and the cry was filled with agony and terror, reverberating hellishly through the churning, hoary fog. I froze there on the slope, chills tumbling along my spine, a sudden vacuum in the pit of my stomach and down low in my groin, and in that moment there was a moaning, a panting, thrashing footfalls in the undergrowth, the sounds of a struggle.

I thought: Holy Christ! And then I thought: Run, get the hell out of here, you don't want any part of what's down there! But then I was straightening up and turning like a damned fool and moving back down the incline, to the sounds, to the flat sandstone rock and the suitcase with three hundred thousand dollars and maybe a boy's life inside it.

My feet sluiced out from under me in my haste, and I landed flat on my back and slid a few feet before I could break my momentum and bring myself up again. I staggered upright, but I could not see anything in the wool-like density of the fog, groping my way blind, and there was another scream, same voice, short and sharp and trailing off in a kind of agonized sigh that was unmistakably the ending of a life, and then the sound of something falling heavily across brittle leafage.

The mist shredded suddenly in front of me and I could see the sandstone rock a couple of feet away on my left, and a black shadow bending over another shadow lying prone near it, and I pulled up short, turning my body toward the shadows and away from the rock, reflex only, not knowing at all what I was going to do, leaving myself unprotected. The bending figure whirled with the tails of a long coat flapping around its knees like folded black wings, and an arm came out and hit me in the stomach, a glancing blow sliding across, but Jesus! he must have had lead in his fist because the pain boils through my belly and I stumble backward and sit down hard and I can see him moving slow-motion away from me, to the rock, hefting the suitcase, moving again, blending with the fog, gone, vanished, and I try to get up but I can't goddamn it he didn't hit me that hard!

I put my hand there as I roll over onto my knees, and I feel wetness and warmth, how can that be, and then

I take my hand away and hold it up to my eyes and it is dripping, dripping dark fluid, and all at once I realize what has happened, I know what it is, *he cut me the son of a bitch cut me he cut me with a goddamn knife!*

And now the fire comes, the searing burning fire, and in my mind I see my entrails exposed to the gray-mold fog, I see my belly ripped open and my guts hanging out and the mist touching them like unwashed surgeon's fingers, I hear a moan low and wailing but it is my voice this time and my guts oh God oh Jesus I'm going to die he cut me and I'm going to die

get up, get up and run but I can't yes I can

my vision all blurry or is that the fog or is that crying, no a man does not cry but the pain, get up

on my feet now, I don't know how, and staggering forward with my hand holding them in and I see the shadow and he is dead with dark fluid leaking out from his belly, a stranger dead with his belly cut open

and I'm running up the embankment, feet sliding, half crazy with the pain and the fear and the fog so cold so dirty is all around me I'm dying you goddamn lousy world I'm alone and I'm dying for what, oh God what happened

the road now and the metal hood of my car like ice, clawing the door, falling inside

oh oh oh the dome light is on and I see the blood the blood oh no please no

the key find the ignition the gear stick

one hand on the wheel and one to hold in my dripping guts

hurtling through grayness and blackness
can't think can't see

sweat in my eyes and the pain you don't know the pain and the blood I'm so frightened
light ahead help help but it's too late I'm dying
look out look out car veering no control and going off look

8

I remembered nothing, and I remembered everything.

Vividly brief scenes with no continuity, like film edited and spliced together by a madman. All in floating, surrealistic white and gray, except for the brilliant red color of blood. And when the reel of film ended, abruptly —only the richest and deepest of blacknesses.

I knew the pain.

Even through the blackness, I knew the pain.

It raged and seethed inside me, and then, sated on my flesh, it grew still and became little more than dull, half-realized throbbings in my stomach and my head. I lay with it, coming out of the velvet midnight, watching the dawn consume the darkness at the edges, and at first I was calm, waiting.

But then the film began again, without warning, and half comatose and half rational, I relived it all and saw the blood, and I was terrified. A voice cried out in rising decibels, and it was my voice, and my hands beat at the air with the frantic flutterings of a wounded bird. Fingers soft and gentle took my arms and stilled them and laid me down again, and something cool and moist brushed with careful strokes across my forehead.

I heard myself whimpering, a child's whimpering, and somehow I managed to stop that. Then the voice that was not my voice, that was too high-pitched and too filled with terror to have been my voice, began crying, "He stabbed me and took the money, I'm dying oh please you have to call Martinetti, Martinetti has to be told about the money!"

The cool, moist strokes continued, and it was a woman's caressing, a woman wearing apple-scented perfume and talking to me in words soft and gentle like her fingers. Some of the panic left me, and I could feel calm returning, and I was aware that I was coming out of it, that I was waking up. I did not want to wake up, because I was afraid of what I would learn, but the panic was no more and with the calm came the need to know. I could not stay under much longer.

My brain began to clear, and it was full dawn soon and the blackness was gone. I lay there, awake now, with only a fuzziness disturbing the clarity of my thoughts, my eyes squeezed tightly shut and my hands pulled into fists at my sides. I knew I was in bed, in a hospital; there were the faint odors of ether and disinfectant and floor wax—institutional smells—pushing away the quiet apple scent of the woman, and knowing this, my body took on a stiffness, a rigidity, and images tried to push their way into my mind. I fought them, I fought them desperately, because they were carefully buried images of things I had seen in field hospitals in the South Pacific, and I knew that if I allowed them to return they would bring the panic and the terrible fear with them. I fought them, and I won, and they retreated. The confrontation left me gasping for breath. I closed my mouth and willed normalcy to my lungs.

I listened. There was a faint, faraway ticking that would be a wall clock, perhaps, and the sounds of hospital activity muted by thick walls, and now the scraping of a chair, and now a muffled cough, and now nothing.

I opened my eyes.

My vision was clear, except for lingering, shimmering pulses of light at the periphery of it. I was looking at a big man in a white hospital smock, with big capable hands and gold-rimmed spectacles and a neat salt-and-pepper mustache. He was smiling, a tired and wan smile, standing just beyond the tubular gray rail at the foot of the bed on which I lay. The walls of the room behind him were a pale green, with an off-white ceiling, and there was a white table with a stainless-steel water carafe and some plastic cups on it.

I looked at the doctor, blinking a little. I said in a calm, clear voice—my voice, "Am I dying?"

"No," he answered gravely, "you're not dying."

I grasped that with my mind, and clung to it, and I saw in his eyes that it was the truth. The quiescence, so tenuous before, now became firm and complete; there would be no more panic. I said, "My belly . . ."

"A nasty cut, but not deep enough to have done much damage. You lost a lot of blood, and it took twenty-seven stitches to close you up, but you'll be all right."

"I thought . . . I thought my entrails were . . ."

"Shock," the doctor said, with a small, understanding nod. "It magnifies things out of proportion. You're not badly hurt, you can believe that."

I let my mind focus on the pain in my stomach now, and it was still dull and vaguely pulsing. They would have used Novocaine as a local anesthetic, and given me some kind of pain-killer, too, which would account for the fuzziness at the fringes of my thinking; the pain perhaps would be stronger later, but I would be able to tolerate it, knowing that I was not dying.

I swallowed into a parched throat, and raised one of my hands off the bedclothes to touch my forehead just over my right eye, where the pain in my head seemed to be centered. I encountered a bandage, with a sensitive lump beneath it. I said, "How did I get this?"

The doctor moistened his lips, and his eyes shifted to my right. For the first time since I had come completely awake, I realized that there were other people in the room. I turned my head on the pillow.

A slender, doe-eyed young nurse stood near the window, auburn hair tucked under one of those little newspaper-sailboat white hats. Her face was solemn and very dedicated, and she would have soft hands and an apple scent about her. In a hard metal chair pulled back from the bed, a very fat man in a dark brown worsted suit sat with his hands flat on his knees. He had shiny black eyes, like smooth Greek olives, and they were watching me with no expression other than a kind of resigned weariness. His mouth was thick and sleepy-looking, and there was a ponderousness to the set of his shoulders, the tilt of his head; but I had worked with cops of one kind and another for a long time, and I knew that that was what he was, and I knew as well that he was not half as soft and sleepy as he appeared or pretended to be.

He shifted a little on his chair and looked at the doctor and the nurse. They left the room immediately, wordlessly. The fat man said to me, "You got the lump when your car went off the road. Steering wheel or windshield. It could have been worse, but you only sideswiped a couple of eucalyptus and nosed into a ditch." He spoke softly and carefully, as if weighing each sentence before putting voice to it.

I said, "Who are you?"

"My name is Donleavy. I'm with the District Attorney's Office of San Mateo County."

I looked at the identification he produced, and moved my head on the pillow in careful acknowledgment. Special investigator. Well, he wouldn't be here if it was just the knife wound in my stomach, I thought—or even if they had only found the dead man by the sandstone rock. But he would have come out, all right, if the authorities had wind of the kidnapping.

Donleavy was watching me think. After a time he said, "Mr. Martinetti is waiting at his home just now, with my partner. If you were wondering whether you should say anything."

"How did you find out?"

"You told us," Donleavy said. "Indirectly."

I just looked at him.

"Man who lives in the house near where you went off the road heard the crash and went out to investigate. He called the hospital here—Peninsula Emergency, if you're interested—and they sent an ambulance. You were delirious when it arrived, kept repeating the name Martinetti and something about a kidnapping and murder and the money being gone. The attendants passed it on to the staff here when they brought you in, and they relayed it to us."

I took a long, slow breath, remembering the shouting I had done in the half-world of returning consciousness. "What time is it now?" I asked Donleavy.

"Just past five A.M."

"Has the boy been released yet?"

"No."

"Any word?"

"No."

"Oh Christ," I said softly.

"Yeah," Donleavy said. "You want to tell me what happened at the drop last night?"

"Do you know the location?"

"Martinetti told us."

"You found the dead man, then."

"Uh-huh. Stabbed in the back, below the right kidney, and cut up deep under the breastbone."

"Who was he?"

"A guy named Paul Lockridge," Donleavy said. "You want to answer some of my questions now?"

"Oh," I said. "I'm sorry."

"Sure."

I told him what had happened, exactly as I remembered it, going over it again to make sure I had left nothing out.

Donleavy said, "And you never saw the guy's face?"

"No. It all happened too fast."

"Did he say anything at any time?"

"No."

"Can you remember anything about him?"

"He wore some kind of long coat."

"What kind?"

"I couldn't tell."

"Is that all?"

"I'm afraid so."

He sighed. "How do you figure it?"

"I hadn't thought that far."

"Well, think that far now."

I pushed it around for several seconds, but my head ached, and I let it go finally and said, "It looks like a double-cross. Two in on the snatch instead of one, and as soon as the money was dropped the killer pulled a knife on this Lockridge. But he wasn't accurate in the dark and the fog, and he just wounded him with the first thrust, in the back. Lockridge screamed and turned and the killer stabbed him under the breastbone, and then I came down in time to get myself cut."

"That's the way it looks, all right," Donleavy said.

"I hope that's not exactly the way it is."

"Why?"

"The boy should have been released by now," I said. "If he was going to be released at all."

Donleavy's forehead wrinkled like the brow of a hound. "A guy uses a knife like that, he hasn't got much conscience or regard for human life, has he?"

"No," I said grimly, "he hasn't."

I lay there and stared down at the top of the tight white bandages ringing my lower stomach, visible through the open front of the cotton hospital gown they had dressed me in. I could feel Donleavy's eyes on me. After a time I said, "How's Martinetti?"

"How would you expect?"

"Yeah."

"He didn't want to talk to us when we went out to his place," Donleavy said. "But he couldn't deny something was wrong, not the way he looked and the way his wife and the others there looked. It was past midnight, and he'd figured things went wrong because you weren't back. We told him what had happened to you as far as we knew it, and he gave us the whole story then. He was a damned fool for not coming to us in the first place with it; if he had, none of this would have happened."

Donleavy's voice had hardened somewhat, but his eyes and his mouth were still sleepy. I said, "You won't get any argument on that."

"Why *weren't* we notified?"

"Martinetti must have told you that."

"I want you to tell me."

"He didn't want the law. He only wanted to pay the ransom to get his son back, to follow the instructions the kidnapper gave him."

"And you went along with that?"

"He didn't ask me for my opinion."

"Maybe you should have offered it."

"It wasn't my place—or my son."

"What *was* your place?"

"To make the drop for him, that's all."

"No investigating, or anything like that?"

"No, just make the drop."

"How much were you getting for that?"

"Fifteen hundred dollars."

"That's nice money for a little drive into the hills."

"And a knife in the belly?"

"You couldn't have foreseen that, could you?"

"Listen, what are you trying to say, Donleavy? That I should have turned down a sour but legitimate job when I could use the money? That I should have violated a client's trust and phoned you people about the kidnapping? That I didn't try to talk Martinetti out of paying the ransom money because that would have meant I'd lose a fifteen-hundred-dollar fee?"

"All of those things crossed my mind."

"And all of them are so much horseshit."

"I've heard of you a little," Donleavy said. "You used to be with the Frisco cops, didn't you?"

"For fifteen years."

"You don't work much, but you've got a decent name."

"Thanks."

"I'm not leaning on you," Donleavy said mildly. He shifted his weight on the chair. "You've been through enough for one night."

I met his eyes. "Look, Donleavy, nobody feels any worse about this whole thing than I do—and I don't mean getting cut. I'm not trying to excuse myself or my actions, right or wrong; I just want you to understand what motivated them, and what didn't motivate them."

"Sure," Donleavy said, and got ponderously to his feet. He sucked in his round cheeks, and puffed them out again, like a blowfish. "We've talked enough for now. I think they want to give you something to make you sleep."

"Will you tell Martinetti what happened?"

"Yeah, I'll tell him."

"All right."

He did that thing with his cheeks again. "I got cut once, in the side, not half as big a gash as you got," he said slowly. "It happened in a bar in Tucson, just after the Korean War; I was new on the cops there and I went up against a guy waving a straight razor. I was never more scared in my life after he slashed me, and I never forgot what happened. I've still got the scar, and every now and then I still get nightmares about it."

He turned, fat but never soft, and shuffled over to the door and opened it and went out without looking at me again. I stared at the ceiling for a while, and then I closed my eyes to rest them. But when I did that, I could see the blood running out between my fingers in the dome light of the car, and I snapped them open again and watched my hands trembling on the bedclothes.

I thought: I'm never going to forget it, either. The scar will see to that. And maybe some nightmares, too, just like the ones Donleavy has every now and then.

9

The doctor and the auburn-haired nurse returned to ask me if there was anybody I wanted notified of my whereabouts. I thought about having them get in touch with Erika, or perhaps Eberhardt, but there was no use in alarming either of them. I said no. They gave me a shot of something then, and I went to sleep almost immediately. I slept deep and hard, and I did not dream. It was one o'clock in the afternoon when I woke up again.

There was no fuzziness to my thinking, and the pain in my head had completely gone; the pain in my belly was no worse than I remembered it being when I had awakened before. But the ingrained fear of hospitals was strong inside me, and I felt claustrophobic. I had to urinate, and I considered throwing back the covers and trying to get up to find the john—but I was afraid to do that on my own because of the stitches. There was a push button attached to the tubular headrest of the bed, and I rang that a couple of times for assistance.

A nurse came in—thin, sad-eyed, flat-chested—and I told her I had to use the toilet but that I wanted to get up and walk there if it was all right. She said it was all right if I was very careful. I got out of bed, leaning on her, and my legs were somewhat weak and the pain grew warm across my lower belly, but I did not fall or stumble when I took my first couple of steps. The nurse went with me out of the room and down the hall one door and waited for me until I came out. Then she walked me back to bed again and wiped the sweat off my forehead with a cloth and patted me as if I had been a very good little boy. She left me alone again.

The claustrophobia had vanished and I lay quiet now. A youngish doctor with an air of nervous energy about him put in an appearance shortly and wanted to know how I felt. I told him. He took the bandages off and examined the wound in my stomach; I did not look at it myself. He put a new dressing on that burned a little, and some more outer wrappings.

I said, "How soon can I get out of here?"

"Perhaps this evening," he answered. "I'll want to look at the wound again before I make it definite."

"Whatever you say."

After he had gone, the flat-chested nurse brought a tray containing some soft-boiled eggs and a cup of luke-warm broth and a dish of liquidy lime jello. I managed to eat some of it.

Oddly, I did not want a cigarette afterward. Oddly, because following any kind of meal, no matter how light, the craving for one was always the strongest. It was the shock of being cut, I supposed, which was responsible for that; my system would be rebelling against such stimulants.

I wondered briefly if my lungs had been examined when they brought me in the night before, as a matter of course, and then decided that it was not likely. I thought: I ought to have them do it while I'm here. I ought to tell them about the cough, and the rasping in my chest, and have them do some X-rays. That's what I ought to do. Well, maybe when the doctor comes again tonight—maybe then I'll tell him.

The door opened and the nurse said, "You have some visitors."

"Who are they?"

"A Mr. Donleavy and a Mr. Reese."

"All right."

Donleavy was still wearing the dark brown worsted; he nodded to me, his expression just as deceptively sleepy as it had been earlier. The other one, Reese, was about thirty, with cool gray-green eyes and flatly stoic features. Sparse, kinky black hair covered his scalp like moss on a round rock. He wore a semi-mod gray suit and a pale gold shirt with a silver-and-black tie, and you got the impression that he thought he was a pretty sharp and urbane guy.

The two of them came over to the side of the bed and pulled up the only two chairs in the room. Donleavy said, "How you feeling?"

"Better."

"This is Ted Reese, my partner."

"Hello," I said.

Reese nodded curtly.

I asked, "Anything new about the boy?"

"No," Donleavy answered. "No calls, no word at all."

Reese said, "We thought you might have remembered something since you talked to Harry last night." His voice was crisp and well-modulated, and had that ring of authority that the younger ones like to affect. I remembered when my own voice had sounded that way, after I had come out of the Police Academy.

I said, "No, I'm sorry."

"Are you sure?"

"I'm afraid so."

"We're not getting anywhere at all," Donleavy said. "We've got to go back and double over everything again."

"What did you find out about the dead guy?"

"His name is Lockridge, like I told you this morning. Home address in Cleveland, wallet with a hundred and twenty-three dollars in it, no credit cards, not much of anything, really, except an Ohio driver's license. No known residence in California, no known next of kin. There was a suitcase in the car we found at the bottom of the slope, but the contents were no help at all; off-the-rack stuff, medium-priced."

"Was he the one who went to Sandhurst and took the boy?"

"Yeah. The headmaster identified a photo of him."

"Did Lockridge have any kind of record?"

"We haven't gotten a report on him yet from the Cleveland police, or from the FBI."

"What about the car?"

"Rental job. The agency couldn't tell us anything about him."

"Prints?"

"Some of Lockridge's, a few others that could belong to anybody, from one of the firm's mechanics to the last renter. We're checking."

"Nothing that could help where it all happened? Footprints, something dropped, like that?"

Donleavy shook his head. "Too many leaves and twigs for footprints. We sifted through the area, but there wasn't anything we could work with."

"Are you going on the assumption that it was somebody in the kidnapping with Lockridge who killed him?"

"We're going on a lot of assumptions right now," he said carefully.

"Okay," I said. "How did Martinetti take the news of what happened?"

"He doesn't blame you for anything, if that was worrying you," Reese said.

"No, it wasn't worrying me." I gave my attention to Donleavy. "Have you let the story out to the papers?"

"Yeah," he said. "Martinetti okayed it this morning. They're going to run a school photo of the boy, and one of Lockridge under a 'Have You Seen This Man?' banner. It'll come out in today's afternoon editions."

"Can you keep the reporters away from me?"

"We've taken care of that. We're not letting them get at the Martinettis either."

"I should think you'd welcome the publicity," Reese said to me, "in your line of work."

"I don't like talking to reporters."

"Let him alone, Reese," Donleavy said mildly. He sighed and got up on his feet. To me: "The doctor tells us you can probably go home tonight, if you take it easy."

"The sooner, the better."

"You'll have to figure out some kind of transportation. We had your car towed into the Harwick Garage in San Bruno, and it'll be there a couple of days at least."

"How bad was the damage?"

"Most of the left side bunged in," Donleavy said. "And you've got a bent A-frame."

I stared down at the foot of the bed. "I guess I'm pretty lucky, all right."

"Yeah, I guess you are."

Reese said pettishly, "You'll be home after you leave here, won't you? In case we want to talk to you again."

"I'll be home."

"And you'll be sure to let us know if you remember something."

"Of course."

Donleavy nodded, and Reese pursed his lips, and they went out.

I lay back and tried to sleep, to keep from thinking about where I was and to make the time pass that much more quickly. But my mind was alert now, and I could not seem to turn it off.

I thought about what had happened at the drop site, and the theory of the double-cross. I could see a flaw in it. Why would Lockridge's partner have chosen to kill him at that particular spot? Why wouldn't he have waited until some later time, when they had the money and were safely away from there? Still, it *was* an isolated location and a body might not be found for some time; it would not be such a bad place to dispose of someone.

Another flaw: why wouldn't he have waited until I was safely gone before using his knife? I had an answer for that one, too, such as it was: he could have gotten excited, thinking about all the money in the suitcase, and decided I was far enough away not to hear anything. He would not have expected to miss a vital spot with that first thrust, and if he had done it right, Lockridge would not have made any sound for me to hear.

But then there was the fact that everything previously had pointed to a single man having engineered the kidnapping of Gary Martinetti. Lockridge was the one who had pulled off the actual abduction of the boy from the Sandhurst Military Academy, and from the voice mannerisms Martinetti had told me about, it seemed as if Lockridge had been the one to make the calls too. The only possible evidence of another party involved in the thing was the warning to Martinetti with the drop instructions: if he, the kidnapper, did not return to a certain place at a certain time, there was someone with the boy who had instructions to get rid of him. But that could have merely been bluff, to insure Martinetti's keeping his end of the bargain.

I could think of one other explanation for last night.

A hijacking.

I touched my tongue to my lips. Well, all right. Somebody who was perhaps not connected with the kidnapping at all, who had found out where the money was to be dropped. Somebody who had waited in the fog and darkness near that flat sandstone rock, watched me deliver the suitcase, seen Lockridge come for it after I had gone, and then gone after him with the knife.

The question there was: how could that somebody have known the exact location of the money exchange? There were two possibilities, one on either end of the spectrum—victim or perpetrator. From Lockridge's side, there existed the chance that he had let the information slip to a girl friend, a relative, a close acquaintance, and that person had taken full advantage of the knowledge. But that did not seem likely; if you're pulling off a capital-offense crime like a kidnapping, you do not talk about it to anyone—and you especially do not reveal the location of the spot where you're getting the ransom money. Lockridge had proven himself very shrewd, very cool in handling the rest of things; a lapse of this kind appeared to be out of character.

From Martinetti's side, only he and I and Proxmire seemingly knew the location of the drop site—but it was likely, even probable, that Karyn Martinetti and Allan Channing and perhaps even the maid, Cassy, could have been told or overheard it. Could one of them have left after I did, taken a shortcut of some kind to get to the hills before I arrived, hidden out by the sandstone rock . . . ?

I did not care for that presumption at all. If one of them had left Hillsborough, the police would have that information by now; that person would be immediately suspect, and would have surely known he would be almost from the beginning; it would be a safe supposition, then, that all of them had been waiting with Martinetti for my return, for the hoped-for telephone call from the kidnapper telling them where the boy could be found.

The only other possibility I could envision along those lines was that one of them had somehow gotten word out of the house to a confederate, relaying to him the drop location. Three hundred thousand dollars was more than sufficient motivation—but were any of them cold enough, corrupt enough, to have jeopardized the life of a nine-year-old boy who was personally close to them to get it? And even if so, that person would obviously have known my mission and the route I would take to reach the drop site; why hadn't his confederate hijacked *me* somewhere along the way instead of waiting for me to deliver the money and leave?

The whole damned thing was a merry-go-round; you could ride it for a long, long time and never even come close to the brass ring. It was no longer any of my concern anyway; I was out of it, legally and morally. This was a business for cops like Donleavy and Reese. They were good men, even Reese; all he needed was a few years in which to learn the subtleties of his profession. And Donleavy was as good as they make them. Whatever there was to be done, to be learned, they would do it and they would learn it.

But I could not seem to get what had happened out of my head. I was too personally involved in it, too close to the core of it; I would carry a scar on my belly and some nightmare memories because of it. There was inside me this kind of frustrated ambivalence of wanting nothing more to do with the affair—and of wanting to see it through personally to its conclusion.

I poured myself a small cup of water from the carafe on the bedside table. I drank a little of it and put the cup down again, and a soft knocking sounded on the door.

A moment later Louis Martinetti came into the room.

I could tell by looking at him that there had been no further word. He appeared skeletal, ghastly, as if all the supporting bones in his body had begun to calcify, so that the features of his face gave the impression of collapsing in on themselves. His eyes were sunken in great purple-shadowed pits, and there were deep excavations beneath his cheekbones. The skin on his lips seemed cracked, perhaps from too much wetting, perhaps from none at all. The iron-gray hair, which had seemed so vital that first time I met him, now looked only brittle and lifeless. He no longer reminded me of the dynamic pulp hero Doc Savage; he reminded me of a man dying as my uncle had died, with something alien and horrible sucking at his flesh from within.

He wore a black suit, black tie knotted loosely over a soiled white shirt. His shoulders drooped, and he walked with a kind of shuffling step, as if his legs were too heavy to lift off the floor. I wondered how long it had been since he had slept—and how long it would be until he slept again.

He sank into one of the chairs beside my bed and rubbed at his face with gray-fingered hands. "They told me it would be all right if I just came in," he said. His voice was that of a hollow man. "They said you weren't hurt as badly as we first thought and that you'd probably be going home tonight."

"Yes."

He made a vague, self-deprecating gesture with his right hand. "I wanted to come earlier, but I thought that I should stay by the phone . . ."

"I understand, Mr. Martinetti."

"My wife and one of the District Attorney's people are waiting now, in case there should be a call." He did not sound as if he believed there would be. "They'll notify me here if they have any news."

There was nothing for me to say.

Martinetti said, "I wanted to talk to you before you went home. I wanted to tell you that I know what happened last night wasn't your fault. You did everything you were humanly able to do, and I appreciate that. More than I can tell you."

His words instilled in me a vague sense of uneasiness. I felt big and awkward and helpless, lying there.

"I know this is a hell of a thing to ask, after what happened to you," he said, "and if you say no, I won't blame you in the least. I spoke to the doctor just before I came in here, and he seems to feel that you'll be able to get around reasonably well after you leave here. That being the case, I'd like you to continue working for me."

I frowned a little at that; I had not anticipated it. "In what capacity, Mr. Martinetti?"

"As an investigator. To help locate my son, and the person who killed this Lockridge."

I released a breath soundlessly through my nostrils. "You already have the facilities of an entire county working toward that same end," I said.

"I realize that," Martinetti said. "But I want every available and competent man possible."

"There isn't anything I can do that the District Attorney's Office isn't already doing."

"You were in on this thing almost from the beginning," Martinetti said. "You have a personal stake in it, after what happened to you."

Those were the same thoughts I had been thinking just before he came in. I said slowly, "Where would I start investigating, Mr. Martinetti? I would only be following in the footsteps of men like Donleavy and Reese by the time I could get on it. And I don't think they'd like that."

"You're allowed to investigate as long as you don't interfere with police actions, aren't you? As long as you report any findings immediately and directly to them?"

"Technically, yes."

"Will you do it, then?"

"I don't know," I said.

He sighed. "Are you aware of the theory the District Attorney's people are pursuing at the moment?"

"Not exactly."

"They seem to think two men were in on the kidnapping of my son, and that one of them killed the other for the money."

"That's a workable theory."

"Yes, but there's another one too. One that they know about, of course, but don't seem to be following at all. One that sickens me, but which nonetheless exists."

"And that is?"

"That someone in my household is responsible for what happened last night," he said.

"Directly, or by collusion?"

"By collusion, of course. They were all present there after you left to deliver the money. But all of them knew, I'm certain, about the location of the money exchange, and any of them could have gotten word to someone on the outside."

"Do you believe that's the case, Mr. Martinetti?"

"It's possible, isn't it?"

"Yes, it's possible."

"Then I'd like you to investigate the theory."

I thought: What am I going to tell him? No, I can't do it—and watch his face crumble even more than it already has, or perhaps pale with frustrated anger? After what happened, did I have the right to turn him down? On the other hand, did I have the right to take his money under what almost amounted to false pretenses—value received for no real value given—and at the same time run the risk of alienation from the local authorities? I did not know what to say; and yet, I had to say something . . .

Martinetti seemed to sense my irresolution. He got slowly to his feet and looked down at me. "Don't give me your answer now. If . . . there's no word on Gary by tonight, I'll call you in San Francisco and you can tell me your decision then. Will that be all right?"

"Yes," I said, and I felt a certain sense of relief. But it was guilt-tinged, because I had taken the easy way out for the moment.

He said, "You'll think about it?"

"I won't be thinking about much else."

"Thank you," he said, and it was a shadow, a pathetic burlesque, of the galvanic Louis Martinetti that I watched shuffle across the room and silently disappear into the corridor outside.

10

Shortly before five a prim little nurse with eyes like two watermelon seeds imbedded in cotton came in and said that there was a telephone call for me, did I feel well enough to walk down the corridor and take it?

I said I felt well enough. She helped me on with a hospital robe, and we walked down to the floor reception desk. There were a lot of patients abroad—old women and old men with death in their eyes, leaning on canes or sitting in wheelchairs or on window benches like fragile and antediluvian artifacts; a tearful young girl immense with child walking on swollen ankles; a portly guy with his face swathed in bandages, making pitiable whimpering sounds as he walked. The scent of fear was strong in that corridor. It was not the consuming fear which had permeated the air inside the war-zone hospitals, but it was potent enough to initiate nausea swirling through my stomach and a kind of weakness at the back of my knees. I had to hold on to the edge of the reception desk for a moment, breathing through my mouth and exerting a conscious effort of will to keep from being violently sick.

"Are you all right, sir?" the nurse asked.

"Yeah," I said. "Just give me a minute."

She watched me uncertainly as I fought down the nausea and the laboredness of my breathing. When I took a couple of steps to where a pay phone with the receiver placed carefully on its lower shelf sat on the adjacent wall, she seemed satisfied that I was not going to keel over on her and moved away.

I caught up the receiver and said hello.

A familiar voice said, very sourly, "Well, you must be in pretty good shape if they let you come to the phone. You goddamn dagos have hide six inches thick."

Eberhardt. I smiled a little. "Thanks for your touching concern, jewboy," I said. The racial jibes were an old thing between us, but they were nothing more than an expression of warmth, of understanding, of comradeship; we had known each other when it was fashionable for the masses to hate and deride the Jews and the Italians along with the other minorities, and we had taken plenty of abuse in our time. We had lived with it, and weathered it, and we had earned the right to make a small joke of it between us. We could relax with our heritage at long last, and God, how nice that was! Maybe there would be a day when this same ease would supplant the bristling hatred extant in some of the other minorities today, and an understanding shrug would replace the stiffened back and the defiantly jutting chin. It would be a fine day if it came.

I said, "How did you hear about it, Eb?"

"I came on at four today," he said, "and there it was on my desk. I thought somebody was pulling a gag at first."

"It's no gag, brother."

"Yeah. How you feeling?"

"Not too bad."

"When they letting you out?"

"Tonight, maybe."

"Jesus," he said, "twenty-seven stitches in the belly," and his voice had gotten softer. He was not nearly as hard or as confirmed a cynic as he liked you to believe; it was a façade, the same way Donleavy's sleepy appearance was a façade. Eberhardt was a good man, a good cop, a good friend; I had been the best man at his wedding twenty-one years ago, and I was his oldest daughter's godfather. I knew that the report on what had happened to me had affected him considerably more than he was letting on.

He said, "Look, as soon as I heard about it and checked with the hospital, I called up Erika and told her. I knew damned well you wouldn't have, and I figured it was better coming from me than from the newspapers."

"I hope you didn't alarm her, Eb."

"How do you sugar-coat a knife in the guts?"

I took a breath. "What did she say?"

"She said she was leaving right away to come down there," Eberhardt said. "She was scared and she was worried, what did you expect?"

"Just that, I guess."

"I'd come down myself if I wasn't on duty."

"I can get along without it."

"Yeah." He was silent for a moment; then: "Listen, take it easy, will you?"

"Don't worry."

He said, "Some chance, a big tough private-eye guy like you," and hung up very gently in my ear.

When I returned to my room, the nervously energetic doctor was waiting for me. He examined my wound, supervised the changing of the dressing, and pronounced me fit to go home—after delivering a list of instructions as to what I could or could not do, eat, and subject myself to.

I asked one of the nurses for the afternoon newspapers, and she brought me copies of the *San Francisco Examiner* and the *San Mateo Times*. The pictures of Lockridge, and the boy in his military uniform, were spread across the front page of both, and the accompanying stories under seventeen-point heads were sketchy and suffered from a lack of salient facts. My name was mentioned twice in the *Examiner*, three times in the *Times*, misspelled once in the latter; I was purported to have been wounded, though not seriously, during the delivery of the ransom money, but my whereabouts were not divulged. I could imagine the number of reporter-placed calls my answering service had gotten in San Francisco, and I wished that the District Attorney's Office had not given out my name at all.

I got out of bed, carefully, because I had developed a restlessness, and went over to the window. I was standing there, watching vacillating threads of gold and burnished brass and coralline interweave on the clear western horizon to fashion the intricate symmetry of an autumn sunset, when Erika arrived at a quarter to six.

She was all in pink—pink scoop-necked shift, pink square-heeled shoes, pink coat with big leather buttons, pink handbag, her hair done up with a pink velvet ribbon in it. She looked twenty-seven instead of thirty-seven. She looked very good.

She came over to me and I kissed her and held her shoulders. Her eyes were deep pools of translucent water, and in them I could read a curious mixture of emotions, some I wanted, some I did not.

"Eberhardt called me," she said. "I had to hear it from him."

"I didn't want to worry you, Erika."

"That's very considerate of you."

"Honey, please, it's not that serious . . ."

"You were almost killed, that's not serious?"

"But I *wasn't* killed," I said. "I'm alive, I'm going to be all right. Isn't that the important thing?"

Her eyes probed mine for a long moment, and then her face softened and she lifted her arms and cupped my face between her palms. "Yes, yes, that's the important thing. Oh God, old bear, it makes me sick inside just to think about you being cut that way, with a knife!" I could feel her shoulders trembling beneath my hands, but she did not cry; Erika had ceased shedding tears in response to a crisis a long time ago.

I drew a long breath, holding her, and then I noticed that in her left hand was a large paper bag with the name of some clothing store on it. I said lightly, "Hey, what'd you bring me?"

"I stopped to buy you some clothes. Eberhardt said yours were . . . ruined and you needed something to get home in . . ."

"Lord, you're a wonder."

"Sure."

I took the bag gently out of her hand and kissed her again and said, "It's time I got out of here, honey. Let's go home."

Twenty minutes later I was dressed in a white

shirt and a pair of flannel slacks and a poplin jacket, checking out at the reception desk. They gave me a statement there, and the amount on it seemed exorbitant at first—but I did not say anything about it; perhaps it wasn't really so much, after all, for my life. The doctor was there with more instructions, and I promised him that I would see a local physician in San Francisco within the next couple of days to have the dressing changed and healing progress on the wound checked. We shook hands, solemnly, like two church deacons at a Sunday social, and then Erika and I went out into the cool night air.

She had a three-year-old beige Valiant, and she drove it like an old lady in an Essex: body rigidly erect, both hands locked on the wheel, the speedometer needle frozen at fifty-five once we got onto Bayshore North at San Bruno Avenue. She made me nervous watching her, and I stared out through the windshield instead, sitting low on the seat with my legs splayed out to ease the constriction in my stomach.

I made a couple of attempts at conversation, but Erika wasn't having any. She had her mouth pulled tight at the corners, and I knew that she was brooding and why she was brooding, and I thought that it was a good thing she wanted silence. I kept on staring out the windshield, trying to decide what I was going to do about Martinetti's offer.

I went over the pros and cons of it a half dozen times, and resolved nothing at all. I knew what I ought to do, and that was to tell Martinetti no when he called, to just wash my hands of the whole thing. And yet, the prospect of doing that made me feel edgy and impotent. I was not a quitter, and to step out of the affair now made me just that; as long as I did not violate any laws, or get in anybody's hair, I had something of an obligation to myself to stay with it until it was concluded, one way or another.

I thought: Well, maybe it will all break by tonight and I won't have to make any decision. I hope that's the way it is; Christ, I hope that's the way it is.

San Francisco was blanketed in fog, and as we left the freeway I could feel a coldness settling on my spine despite the warmth of the car's heater. The shredded gray tendrils of mist recalled last night and its violent chain of events vividly to my mind; I shivered a little, and the pain grew gnawing across my lower belly.

There was a parking space almost directly in front of my building, for a change, and Erika spent three minutes putting the Valiant into it. She came around and took my arm as I got out of the car, holding on to it tightly, and we went up onto the porch. The police and the hospital staff had gathered my personal effects from the blood-soaked ruin of my own clothing. When I used my key on the front door and my apartment door, I was breathing only just a little heavily from the climbing of the single flight of stairs.

Erika let her eyes wander with distaste over the living room as we stepped inside. She said, "My God, how can you stand to live like this?" But there was a lightness to her words, the first she had spoken since we'd left the hospital, that gave the impression of relaxation inside her now. She had finished her brooding, having apparently come to some conclusion or resignation; the tightness was gone from the corners of her mouth, and she was beautiful and soft for me again.

I said, "You say the same thing every time you come here."

"It doesn't seem to do any good."

"Can I help it if I'm a slob at heart?"

"Oh, go lie down, will you?" she said. "I'll fix you something to eat. Are you hungry?"

"Sure."

"Well, that's a good sign anyway."

Erika took off her coat and went over and hung it up in the coat closet. Then she disappeared into the kitchen and clicked on the lights and made an exasperated sound and began banging pots and things around. I walked to the couch and swept some newspapers onto the floor and lay down.

There was a package of cigarettes on the coffee table, and I looked at it and thought about having one. But the craving was not at all strong, and I did not want to provoke Erika into any kind of argument. Besides that, I had a running start on quitting them now, the kind of start I would not have again; if I was going to do it at all, this was the right time.

I picked up the copy of *Black Mask* that I had been reading two nights ago, and began to thumb idly through it. I started to glance over the story I had begun then, without any real hope of being able to concentrate, but the opening gripped me this time and I was ten pages involved in it when Erika came in with a tray a few minutes later.

She put the tray down on the coffee table, clearing away some of the dishes and things. She said, "Don't you ever tire of reading those silly magazines?"

"No," I said. "Don't you ever tire of cleaning up?"

"What do you think?"

"You'll make some guy a good wife anyway."

"I can give you the names of two guys who wouldn't agree with that," she said.

"A hell of a lot they know."

"Maybe they know best of all."

"Nuts," I said. I looked at the tray. There was some beef broth and a fluffy omelette and a dish of applesauce. It wasn't the kind of stuff I liked to eat as a rule, but I sat up dutifully and put the pulp aside and went to work on the food.

I was halfway through the meal when the telephone rang. I looked up at the sunburst clock over the false fireplace; it was eight-thirty. I said to Erika, "Answer that, will you, honey? If it's Louis Martinetti, I'll talk to him. Nobody else."

She looked at me sharply, and then went into the bedroom and cut off the phone in mid-ring. I heard her tell somebody that I wasn't available for comment just now, she was sorry, and a moment later she came back into the front room. "Somebody from the *Chronicle*," she said.

I finished the meal she had prepared, and Erika took the tray away and came back and began to clean up. I lay down again and tried to read some more of the *Black Mask* story, but it was no good now. I was tense and waiting for Martinetti's call, because I knew what I was going to tell him; I had known it the instant the telephone rang before and I had thought it might be him.

He called at five to nine.

Erika went in to answer it, and returned with the phone on its long cord. She gave it to me, mouthing Martinetti's name silently, and went away into the kitchen. I said, "Yes, Mr. Martinetti?"

"There's nothing yet," he said, "nothing at all." Even over the wire, his exhaustion was plainly evident. "I've just heard from the District Attorney's people."

"Then you still want me to keep working for you."

"Yes. Will you do it?"

I blew a soft breath away from the mouthpiece. "All right, Mr. Martinetti. I'll do what I can. But I want you to understand that it probably won't be much, and that I don't want any money unless I make some kind of contribution."

"Whatever you wish," he said.

"Call me at any time if you have some news. If I don't hear from you, I'll know there aren't any further developments."

"Yes." He was silent for a moment, and then he said, "I . . . I appreciate this. More than I can tell you."

"Sure," I said. "I hope I can help, Mr. Martinetti."

We said goodbye and I replaced the handset in its cradle. I sat there and looked at the phone and I felt better about it all now, having reached a decision. I turned away to lie down again and Erika was standing just behind the couch with the tightness back at the corners of her mouth and her eyes very dark.

I said, "You were listening."

"Yes, I was listening," softly, flatly.

"Erika . . ."

"You damned fool," she said in sibilant tones, "oh, you poor damned fool. You can't let it alone, can you? You've got to stay right in there until the bitter end."

"Look," I said, "you don't understand . . ."

"Don't I? I understand very well, you'd be surprised what I understand. I understand that you've got a knife wound in your stomach from this business, this skulking around in the night, and now you want to keep right on with the case. Can't walk out on a client, isn't that the way it goes? Well, maybe next time the man with the knife won't miss. Maybe next time he'll kill you and you'll die gloriously in the name of truth and right and justice."

"For Christ's sake, Erika . . ."

"No, you hear me out," she said. "I'm going to say what's on my mind, what's been on my mind for a long time now. I'm fed up, old bear. I'm fed up with waiting around for you to change, for you to grow up. I'm fed up with this private-detective business of yours, this cloak-and-dagger crap, this pointless losing proposition that you cling to so damned tenaciously. You haven't had ten clients this year, and yet you go down to that musty-dusty office of yours every morning and you sit there and wait fot the telephone to ring like some character in one of those pulp magazines you collect."

I could feel the anger beginning inside me, and my stomach throbbed painfully now. But it was impotent anger, because there was nothing for me to say to her, no way to make her understand.

She kept on with it. She said, "You want to know the real reason you quit the police force to open up that agency of yours, the real deep-down reason? I'll tell you: it was and is an obsession to be just like those pulp-magazine detectives and you never would have been satisfied until you'd tried it. Well, now you've tried it, for ten years you've tried it, and you just don't want to let go, you *can't* let go. You're living in a world that doesn't exist and never did, in an era that's twenty-five-years dead. You're a kid dreaming about being a hero, and yet you haven't got the guts or the flair to go out and be one; you're too honest and too sensitive and too ethical, too affected by real corruption and real human misery to be the kind of lone wolf private eye you'd like to be. You're no damned hero, and it hurts you that you're not, and that's why you won't let go of it. And the whole while you're eating and sleeping and living yesteryear's dream world, to salve your wounded pride you're deluding yourself that you're an anachronism in a real-life world that couldn't care less one way or the other. You're nothing but a little boy, and I'm damned if I'll have a little boy in my bed every night of the year. That's the reason I wouldn't and I won't marry you; I can't compete with an obsession, I won't compete with it—"

Abruptly she stopped, face flushed with the passion of her words, her gray eyes flashing and silvery with what may have been tears. Then she turned and ran over to the closet and got her coat out. I struggled up onto my feet, but before I could reach her she had the door open and I could hear her shoes clicking on the stairs going down. A moment later the front door slammed and there was only silence.

I stood listening to the echo of her words in my ears, the cutting sting of them. No, I thought, no, she's wrong, she's all the way wrong, that's not the way it is, Jesus, that's just not the way it is!

I went back to the couch and sat there with the pain hot and sharp now in my stomach, staring over at the door. I said aloud, to break the deepening silence, "She'll be back. She didn't mean any of it, not that way."

The words sounded uncertain, supplicating, in the suddenly cold and shabby room.

11

The next morning I awoke feeling stiff and sore. There was a dull throbbing in my temples, and a sharp ache at the center of the lump on my forehead. I went into the bathroom and looked at myself in the mirror; the face that stared back at me was an unhealthy gray and etched with too many lines and crags, like a contour map of an arid and desolate terrain. The whites of my eyes had a rheumy look to them—dull green agates floating in partially curdled milk—and my lips were puffed and dry. The beard stubble on my chin and patterned thickly across my cheeks was the color of old pewter.

I took four aspirins out of the bottle in the medicine cabinet and swallowed a little water with them, and shaved, and passed the toothbrush over the smoke stains on my teeth, and combed my gray-streaked hair, and studied myself again, critically, in the mirror. I did not look or feel much better. I walked back into the bedroom and sat on the bed and stared at the backs of my hands. They were deeply veined and faintly gray. You and Martinetti, I thought. A couple of sick, tired old men—but he would recover after a while, because that was the kind of man he was; nothing would ever completely destroy his vitality, his vigor, his youth. But what about you, tiger? Yeah, what about you?

I stripped off my pajamas and looked at the bandages to see if there was any trouble with the wound. They were clean and dry. I began to dress, slowly and carefully, in one of my two remaining suits—a charcoal worsted that was four years old and had a faint shine along the seat of the trousers. I put on the white shirt Erika had bought, and tied a knitted green tie and fastened it to the shirt with a gold bar clasp. I had just gotten that accomplished when the telephone rang.

I thought it might be Martinetti, but it was, instead, Allan Channing. I frowned a little as he identified himself; his voice was cold and angry and precise.

He said, "I'm calling to let you know that I think Lou Martinetti made a very grave error in judgment in hiring you as an investigator after what happened the other night. You've caused enough trouble as it is."

You supercilious son of a bitch, I thought. I said, "Is that supposed to be some kind of warning, Mr. Channing?"

"Call it what you like," he said. "I hold you personally responsible for what happened to my money, and if it isn't recovered, I fully intend to take steps to see that you don't have the opportunity to inflict similar damages on other individuals. Do I make myself clear?"

"Perfectly," I said between clenched teeth.

"Lou Martinetti is a very good friend of mine,

even if he is prone to irrational ideas and decisions at times, and I don't want any further fumblings in his behalf. I suggest you call him immediately and resign from his employ."

"It must be hell to be a man like you, Channing," I said. "It must be pure hell to value a sum of money more than the life of a nine-year-old boy."

"Listen here—" Channing began.

"Nuts to you, brother," I said, and I slammed the phone down in his ear.

I stood there shaking a little. The bastard, the soulless bastard. I went over and sat down on the bed again and after a while the trembling subsided and I was all right. I got up, and the telephone bell sounded again.

It was Dana Eberhardt this time, wanting to know how I felt and if I needed anything. She was one of the most maternal women I had ever known, and she had been fussing over me for twenty years. She had tried to marry me off to half of her eligible female relatives at one time or another, and it was a great source of frustration for her that she had never even come close to succeeding. A running joke between Eberhardt and me was that if she ever found out I had spent a weekend with her cousin Jeannie in Carmel six years ago, she would bring out a shotgun and march Jeannie and me to the nearest altar.

I assured Dana that I was all right, and that I would take care of myself and that I would come up to see them the first chance I got. I wished she had not found out what had happened, because the chances were that I would never hear the end of it. She and Eberhardt were as bad as Erika, in their own way, when it came to my profession.

Erika. I looked at the phone, thinking that I wanted to talk to her—and yet I did not want to talk to her. I could still feel the unfair bite of her words last night. But I would be needing the use of a car today, and she kept hers in a lot on Mission Street, not far from my office.

I dialed the number of her firm in the financial district, and the switchboard there put me through to her. "Well," she said, "how nice." Her voice was cool. "You sound very fit this morning. Did you sleep well?"

"I slept fine," I lied. "Listen, Erika, I called to ask if I could borrow your car today."

Silence. I counted mutely to eleven, and then she said, "Is that all you wanted?"

"For now, yes."

"I'll call the garage for you, then," she said flatly. "You won't get any blood on the upholstery, will you? If you're stabbed again, or shot, I mean."

"That's not funny, Erika."

"It wasn't intended to be," she said, and she broke the connection with a soft click.

I took a taxi down to the parking garage on Mission and picked up the Valiant and drove it over to Taylor Street. My office was in the Kores Building, a couple of blocks off Market, and I parked perversely in a yellow loading zone a half-block away. The sun was out by then —it was after ten—but there was a chill autumn wind blowing through the concrete-and-steel canyons of the city. I walked as quickly as I thought it wise to be walking, my hands shoved down in the pockets of the heavy tweed topcoat I had put on before leaving my apartment.

The entrance to the Kores Building was nothing more than a narrow doorway wedged between a dealer in old coins and a luncheonette. I went inside, and the lobby was as it always was: cold and dark and still. I checked the row of tenants' mailboxes, found mine empty, and then took the elevator up to the third floor.

My office smelled of dust and stale cigarette smoke. I went over and opened the window behind my desk a little, letting in the traffic noise from Taylor Street below. Then I knelt down gingerly by the steam radiator and fiddled with the controls and listened to the pipes banging somewhere in the bowels of the building.

A hot plate rested on the top of the single metal file cabinet, and I went there and lifted the lid on the coffee pot sitting on it and looked inside. A faint greenish substance had gathered around the edges of the coffee I had made three mornings ago. I carried the pot into the alcove on the right-hand side of the single room, washed it out in the sink, and made some fresh. After I had plugged in the hot plate, I sat behind the desk in my overcoat, listening to the ringing knock of the radiator, waiting for it to warm up and for the coffee to boil. The clock on the wall above the file cabinet read 10:37.

I picked up the phone and called my answering service. There were no messages from anyone I cared to call back. I thanked the girl and told her I would be in for a while.

The coffee began bubbling. I got up again and poured some into a clean cup and carried it back to the desk. I stared at the steam rising in faint curling wisps and wondered where I was going to start today.

Martinetti had not called, and that meant there were still no further developments. I did not particularly care for the idea of driving down to Hillsborough and facing the pall of gloom that would be the Martinetti household, but that seemed to be the only logical way of approaching an investigation. I could talk to each of the people there, do a little circumspect probing . . .

The sound of the knob turning and the door being pushed open caught and held my attention, and I watched with some surprise the harried form of Dean Proxmire step into the office.

He wore a belted tan trenchcoat, stylish and nicely cut, and there was some color in his hollowed cheeks from the stinging wind. His lips were pursed into a thin horizontal line, and his deeply hooded eyes told me that he was nervous and very tired, and perhaps just a little unsure of himself. He shut the door, looked at me, looked away, and let his gaze flicker over the office: the pale papered walls and the pebbled-brown asphalt tile floor; the old leather couch outside the low rail divider, set beneath a framed photograph of my license and a photograph of my graduating class at the Police Academy; three chairs and a small table with a dusty glass ashtray on it and some magazines that nobody had ever read; the file cabinet, of a somber gray metal, sharing the wall beyond the alcove with the steam radiator and a four-color calendar featuring a sunset on bucolic meadows; the second-hand oak desk with its cluttered surface and the coffee cup sitting in the middle of the memo blotter and me behind it watching him steadily.

Proxmire took it all in very slowly, and what he saw seemed to give him some assurance. He put his eyes on my face and left them there and walked purposefully through the gate in the divider and over in front of the desk. I got up on my feet because I did not want him talking down to me in any way. I said, "Good morning, Mr. Proxmire."

"Is it?" he said stiffly.

I let that pass. "What can I do for you?"

"I understand you've consented to do some investigating for Mr. Martinetti."

I shrugged noncommittally.

"Well, I should think after what happened to you, you'd want no more part in this business," he said. "I should think you'd be damned glad to have gotten out of it with your life."

"Which means what, Mr. Proxmire?"

"Just what I said."

"I take it you don't like the idea of my continuing on the case in an investigative capacity."

"Frankly, I don't like it at all."

"Why?"

"Would you like the flat truth?"

"Of course."

"I have my doubts as to your competency," Proxmire said. The belligerence in his voice seemed a little forced.

"Is that right? Would you mind telling me the reason?"

"That should be obvious."

"Martinetti doesn't blame me for what happened two nights ago."

"Listen," Proxmire said, "I don't like the idea of someone like you snooping around. God knows, we've got enough problems just now, what with no word on Gary . . ."

"*We*, Mr. Proxmire?"

His cheeks seemed to gain more color. "The Martinettis, I meant."

I said, "And just what did you mean by 'snooping around'?"

"You know perfectly well what I meant," Proxmire said. "Martinetti has some damn-fool notion that someone who was in his house the day of the ransom delivery is responsible for what happened to you, for murdering the kidnapper, Lockridge. And he wants you to check up on us."

"You don't care for that theory, I take it?"

"No, I don't!" Proxmire said emphatically. "It's plainly ridiculous. The District Attorney's people seem to feel it was a partner of this Lockridge, and that's what I think too."

"What harm can it do to check all the possibilities?"

"It's a waste of time and money."

"My time and Mr. Martinetti's money," I said. "Why should that bother you so much?"

"Damn it—"

"Or are you worried about what an investigation might turn up? Do you have something to hide, Mr. Proxmire?"

A tic had gotten up under his left eye, and it made the lower lid jump spasmodically. He said, too quickly, "Of course not! What would I have to hide?"

I shrugged. "I couldn't say."

"Are you insinuating I had something to do with what happened?"

"I'm not insinuating anything at all," I said. "You came to me, Mr. Proxmire, remember that."

"Listen here, I won't have you asking a lot of personal questions and upsetting everyone at a time like this!

Mrs. Martinetti is on the brink of total collapse . . ." He broke off, as if he had realized that he might be telling me just a little too much in an indirect way. I could hear the click of his teeth as he clamped his mouth tightly shut.

I said quietly, "I don't have any intention of upsetting anyone. And the only things I'm interested in are those that might pertain to the chain of events involving the kidnapping. Whatever else I might know or happen to find out is irrelevent to the job I was hired for; I don't intend to make use of it in any way at all."

We stood there staring at one another. The tic under Proxmire's eye caused him to avert his head finally, and as soon as he did that he turned around and went over to the door. He looked back at me just before he went out, and there were a plethora of emotions mirrored on the gaunt planes of his face. He was a man under a severe strain—not the kind of strain Martinetti was under, perhaps, but one which could be just as damaging internally. I listened to his footsteps retreating along the hallway outside.

I sat down again. It was a nice morning so far: first Channing, and now Proxmire, who did not want me doing any specific investigating for Martinetti. One because he stood to lose three hundred thousand dollars of his money and needed someone to blame for it, and the other because he was having an affair with, and was apparently in love with, Louis Martinetti's wife. Or were the motivations even deeper than that? Was Proxmire, or maybe Channing, afraid I would discover something else . . . ?

Well, that kind of speculation was useless at this point. I drank some more coffee and thought that I wanted a cigarette; but there were none in the office, and I would have to go downstairs and over to the luncheonette to get a package. I did not feel like doing that. It was probably just as well, because I had the habit licked by two days now, and the first couple were always the hardest, wasn't that what they always told you?

The telephone rang.

I looked at it and wondered if it was a reporter, and thought that if it was I would hang up on him. I caught up the receiver and gave my name, and a very small, very timorous, almost inaudible feminine voice said haltingly, "Are . . . are you the detective who is involved with the Martinetti kidnapping?"

I took the receiver away from my ear and frowned at it and put it back and said, "Yes, that's right. Who's calling, please?"

"I . . . I'd rather not give my name. You wouldn't know me anyway."

"Well, what was it then?"

"I called you because I . . . I think I might know something about that . . . that man."

"Lockridge? The dead kidnapper?"

"Yes, him."

"The people you want are the police, lady—"

"No!" She said it very fast, raising her voice above the whisper, and then quickly dropped it down again: "No, I . . I don't want the police. I . . . won't talk to them. Not yet."

"Why not?"

"I have my reasons."

"But you'll talk to me."

"I . . . yes."

"If you'll give me your address . . ."

"Oh no," she said, "no, I won't do that. You'll have to meet me. Alone."

Christ, I thought. You could suffocate under all this heavy melodrama. "All right. Where?"

"Do you know the section of Golden Gate Park where they have the Portals of the Past?"

"I know it, yes."

"I'll meet you at the first portal near the drive, at twelve. I . . . I won't come near you if you're not alone."

"I'll be alone."

"I hope you are," she said, and that was all.

I sat staring at the dead phone, and then put it back in its cradle very carefully. I looked up at the clock on the wall, and it was past eleven now. There was not enough time to contact the District Attorney's Office of San Mateo County and have Donleavy or one of their other men get up here. I could call Eberhardt, but there did not seem to be much sense in it; the woman could be, and probably was, a crank after all. If not, however, if she did know something important and she thought I wasn't completely alone, I would be running the risk of losing her altogether.

It was mine to follow through, something or nothing.

12

It was very cold in Golden Gate Park.

I parked Erika's Valiant on John F. Kennedy Drive, directly opposite the shallow expanse of Lloyd Lake around which the Portals of the Past were located, and got out into an icy wind blowing harsh over the all but deserted lawns and trees and paths of the park. I pulled the collar on the overcoat up around my neck and bunched my shoulders inside the heavy garment and walked across the empty roadway to where a narrow dirt path skirted the lake's left bank.

Overhead, the coldly pale sun was visible through an approaching haze of fog. Reflections of light danced on the surface of the lake, interspersing patches of translucent blue on the leaden patina of the calm water. On the far bank, to the right of where the lake turned into the mouth of a tiny green valley, a narrow waterfall bubbled whitely over a rock stairway.

Ducks, like playful toys, floated on the surface of the lake, making no sound. A lushly grown slope capped with fanning, stilted cypress trees paralleled the path on my left; great bushes of chrysanthemum grew there, and ringed the lake at intervals—explosions in white, tipped in pink.

I followed the lane until I reached the first portal, a tall marble-and-stone affair with a stone bench set into the arch. The bronze plaque at the base said that it was the Portal of Residence of A. N. Towne, Vice-President and General Manager of Southern Pacific Railroad, a relic of the conflagration of April 18, 1906.

I sat down on the bench, carefully, with my legs splayed out in front of me like a pregnant woman's in deference to the healing wound in my belly. My watch said that it was a couple of minutes before twelve. I pressed my hands deep into the pockets of the overcoat and sat there with the wind blowing cold across my face, watching the ducks floating woodenly on the lake's glasslike surface. It was all very peaceful, almost pastoral, in its serenity.

I thought with philosophical cynicism: My own private Walden Pond—except that it isn't mine and it isn't private, it's nothing more than nature compressed by manmade structures on all sides, nature reduced to a small and inexorably diminishing sanctuary that will, someday, be swallowed and digested in the name of that sterile, soulless, meaningless term Progress.

And then I stopped thinking thoughts like that, because they never got you anything in the long run except manic-depressive, and turned my head toward the road to watch for the woman's approach; if she was coming at all, she would probably come from the east or west along there.

A couple of cars went by, and a young couple in matching green trenchcoats and heavy mufflers, trailing a black Scotch terrier on a chain leash. A few seagulls flew overhead, adding raucous cries to the humming lament of the wind. Twelve o'clock came and went, and it got colder sitting there on the bench; my fanny felt as if it were planted in a block of ice.

12:10.

I'll give her another five minutes, I thought, and that's all. I did not think it was a good idea for me to be out in the cold like this, with that wound the way it was; I had heard somewhere that you were especially susceptible to pneumonia when you had been injured, and that would be all I needed just now.

I shifted my chilled feet and touched my tongue to my wind-chafed lips, and then I saw her come into view from beyond the slope at my back, walking hesitantly along Kennedy Drive. She looked over at me, and paused, and walked on a little way and stopped and looked over at me again. She was making up her mind. I sat there without moving, letting her reach a decision, and finally she came over to where the path began and started toward me with these little hesitant steps, head bobbing up and down as she moved like a bird approaching an unfamiliar feeder.

She wore a heavy blue shag coat with huge dark-wood buttons, and a lighter blue scarf over her hair and knotted under her chin. A pair of gray tweed slacks peeked out at the bottom of the coat. As she came closer, I could see that she was maybe twenty-six or -seven, very thin, very pale. Wispy bangs were visible beneath the scarf: a lusterless brown.

She stopped when she was about twenty feet away and stood there as if she expected me to jump up and make a rush at her. When I didn't move, it seemed to reassure her; she came forward finally, with a kind of resolution, and stood in front of me.

She said, "You're the detective?"

"Yes, ma'am," I answered.

"Are you alone?"

"Yes."

She looked around with a furtiveness that was almost a theatrical burlesque. Her eyes were wide and wet and colorless, slightly protuberant under all but nonexistent lashes, and her mouth was a pale oval in the marmoreal cast of her face. She looked like the stereotyped conception of a small-town maiden librarian.

Her gaze came back to me again and she said, "Is it all right if I sit down there with you?" a little breathlessly.

"Of course." I moved over, and she seated herself with her knees together and flattened the skirts of her shag coat over her knees with the palms of thin, very white hands.

"I . . . I guess you think I'm a little crazy, asking you to meet me like this," she said.

"I imagine you have your reasons."

"I just don't want to . . . to make any rash decisions, that's all. I mean, I don't want the police to have anything to do with this until I make up my mind what's right."

"You said you knew something about the man who kidnapped the Martinetti boy," I said. "Paul Lockridge."

"Yes, well, I think so," the librarian said. "I mean, I'm not sure. Not really sure."

"What is it you're not sure of, Miss—?"

She did not fall for that. She said, "You must understand, I'm just not *sure*. If I was . . . well, that poor little boy, I wouldn't want anything to happen to a little boy."

"I'm certain you wouldn't."

She took a long, quavering breath. "I think this Lockridge is the man my sister has been . . . seeing for the past few weeks."

"Your sister?"

"Yes. She's two years younger than I am, and a little . . . well, a little wild. We share an apartment, and one night this fellow came around to pick her up for a date and I think . . . it might have been Lockridge. I mean, I only saw him that one time but I think he's the man."

"Have you spoken to your sister about this?"

"No. But she's very frightened about something, I can tell. She's really very frightened. She's been . . . away for several days, and when she finally came home this morning she was terribly nervous and upset."

"Where had she been?" I asked.

"I don't know that," the librarian said. "I asked her, but she wouldn't tell me."

"Is your sister at your apartment now?"

"Yes."

"Does she know you're here with me?"

"No. I didn't want her to know, not before I talked to you. There are some things I want to be sure of before I say anything to her."

"And that's why you called me," I said.

"Yes."

I looked off at the lake for a moment. The ducks were still floating on its surface, quietly motionless. A couple of gulls buzzed them like P-51's after a ground target, and they sat there with the cool imperturbability of middle-aged spinsters at afternoon tea. The gulls flew off, screaming obscenities into the wind.

I looked again at the librarian and said, "What kind of things did you expect me to tell you?"

"She's never been in trouble before, you know. Never. She's a good girl, really. What . . . what would happen to her if she just made this one mistake and got involved with the wrong kind of man?"

"Not much, maybe," I said. "It would depend on the extent of her involvement."

"I think she was . . . in love with this man. Love is blind, isn't that what they say?"

"Yeah," I said. "That's what they say."

"She couldn't have known very much about the kidnapping," the librarian said. "Not Lorraine . . . I mean, not my sister, no."

"If she gives herself up, voluntarily, things could go fairly easy for her. She might even get off with nothing more than a probationary slap on the wrist."

"Do you really think so?"

"It would be up to a judge, of course."

"But the chances would be good, wouldn't they?"

"They would be, yes," I said, "assuming that nothing has happened to the boy. That he's returned unharmed to his parents."

A look of infinite horror blanched her already white face the color of bright snow. "Well, of course he's all right! Lorraine would never . . . oh my God, no, no, he's fine, he must be!"

"Look," I said, "why don't you take me to her? Maybe I can—"

"No, I don't want you to see her! Not yet. Please,

I have to do this my own way. I have to talk to her first, don't you see?"

I just looked at her.

"She's my *sister*," the librarian said in this tiny, fierce voice. "I don't want her hurt or frightened any more than she already has been. I want to help her."

"Listen," I said, "there's a little boy missing. He may be sick or hurt, and he's almost surely a hell of a lot more frightened than your sister. He's got a family down in Hillsborough, torn apart by grief and tension, sitting by the telephone and waiting and not hearing anything. What do you think it's like for them, for that boy, while you sit around making up your mind what to do?"

"Lorraine is *my* family! The only family I have!" There were tears in her colorless eyes now, glistening, but the steadfast determination was strong in them nonetheless. "I can't . . . I can't just turn her over to the police! Not without being absolutely sure. Don't you think I've thought about that little boy? Don't you think I've gone through hell since I first saw those pictures in the paper last night?"

"All right," I said, and I made my voice softer, gentler. I was running the risk of alienating her completely, and the more I watched her, the more I listened to her, the more I felt that what she was telling me was the truth; she was not a crank, and she was not the type who saw menace under every lamppost and disaster in every ringing of the telephone. Her concern for her sister was consumingly and unshakably genuine; in spite of her earlier protestations, she was as positive as could be that Lockridge was the guy who had been dating Lorraine, and that Lorraine, by her actions, knew something about the kidnapping.

I said, "What is it you want to do now? Go back home alone and talk to your sister? Try to find out for certain if she's involved?"

"Yes, that's what I want."

"And if she is, then what?"

"Why . . . why, we'll come to you, Lorraine and I," she said. "And the three of us will go to the police together."

"That's fine," I said quietly, "but suppose she doesn't want to go to the police? Suppose she runs away instead?"

"No!" the librarian said positively. "No, she wouldn't do that."

"You're absolutely sure?"

"Yes!"

"If you're wrong, and she does run away, you could be sent to prison for aiding and abetting a felon—as an accessory after the fact in the commission of a major crime. Have you thought about that?"

"I don't care about myself! Lorraine won't run away, so it doesn't matter. I know my sister, she wouldn't do that!" She jumped up onto her feet. "I made a mistake calling you! I shouldn't have called anyone!"

"Take it easy," I said. "Just take it easy now."

"I'm not carrying any identification," she said grimly. "If you think you can take me to the police and make me tell you who I am and where Lorraine is, I won't say a word. I won't, I mean that!"

"I'm not going to try to take you anywhere," I said. "You can handle it however you want to. I'll go along with your wishes."

Some of the defiance went out of her eyes. "You will? You'll let me do this my way?"

"Yes, however you want to do it."

"It's the best way, it really is."

"If you think so, all right."

"I'll go to Lorraine right now. I'll tell her what you said, and if . . . if she's really involved she'll listen to reason."

"I hope she will."

"Oh yes, yes, she will."

"Okay, then."

"I'll call you after I've talked to her," the librarian said. Her hands moved like thin white spiders along the front of her coat. She was not half as convinced of her sister's reasonableness as she tried to make out, but she did not want me to know that. "I'll call you at your office, and we'll come there and meet you. Will that be all right?"

"Yes, that's fine," I said.

"It won't be long, really it won't."

"I'll be waiting for your call."

"Thank you . . . thank you." She smiled, tentatively, fleetingly, and it was ghastly in the ivory pallor of her face. "You're very understanding. You are, you know."

I said nothing.

She pivoted and started along the path, moving with that birdlike motion of her head and those quick little steps. She went twenty yards and stopped and whirled around, and I was still sitting there watching her. Her head jerked frontally again and she walked to the road and stopped and looked back at me with a surreptitious motion that might have been humorous in another situation. I had not moved. She turned to the right, west on Kennedy Drive, and disappeared from sight past the densely grown slope.

I kept on sitting there, trying to hold down the sense of urgency that was growing deep inside me and making the knife wound throb with a muted intensity. I thought: Foolish little girl, loyal little girl, goddamn naïve little girl! I was sorry for her, and sad for her, and it did not help to know that I was going to betray her. But there were bigger evils, stronger motives and emotions, involved here; her problems, her fears, were going to be swallowed and absorbed the way life seemed to have swallowed and absorbed her—completely and mercilessly—from the very beginning. It was the cold, hard way of things.

I had to give her some time, some assurance that she was not being followed; she would be stopping every twenty or thirty yards to look over her shoulder. I let her have another minute, and that was all the waiting I could take. I got up and walked as quickly as I was able near the end of the path and stepped off it and went to where I could look beyond the slope at the gentle curve of the drive. She was nowhere in sight.

The urgency grew stronger. Christ, I thought, maybe I waited too long at that. I moved in a half-running, half-shuffling gait across the roadway and got into the Valiant and started it and took it forward. As I drove, my eyes roamed both sides of the drive for some sign of that distinctive blue coat and scarf. If she had cut south across the rolling verdant lawns toward Metson Lake or Elk Glen Lake or the Golden Gate Park Stadium, I should have been able to see her; but the wind-swept, leaf-strewn greensward was void of humanity.

Ahead on the right, the narrow Marx Meadow Drive angled back behind Lloyd Lake and the Portals of the Past, to join eventually with the cross-over from 25th Avenue that emptied into the main north-south boulevard,

Park Presidio. I looked along there as I passed it, but it appeared to be empty. Damn! She could have gone onto any one of the numerous paths winding through the trees and thick undergrowth on the right, honeycombing the area and leading on a dozen street exits. And yet, the librarian had not seemed like the type to go wandering through the cold, dark wood, even in the middle of the day; she would want to stay on the main, traveled areaways as much as possible . . .

I saw her then.

I came around a shallow curve, and she was walking in a diagonal trajectory across the expanse of lawn to the north, to where 30th Avenue came timidly into the park and blended into Kennedy Drive. She walked with surprising quickness in that odd way of hers, head bobbing forward into the wind, not looking back now. She had apparently satisfied herself that I was not going to follow her.

I drove up to where I could see the length of 30th and pulled off on the side of the drive and sat there slouched down with the motor running. If she looked back again, she would not see much of anything out of the ordinary; she would have expected any trailing of her to be done on foot.

I watched the blue shag coat exit the park on Fulton Street. She paused there and looked back quickly, and then crossed the street and continued along 30th Avenue, north. I took the Valiant out of neutral and swung it around and drove up to Fulton and waited between the stone cairns there until the light flashed green. I drove across and pulled over to the curb and watched her span Cabrillo, heading in the direction of George Washington High School.

I stayed at the curb until she was midway in the

second block before pulling out and passing over Cabrillo to the curb again on the other side. She turned left on Balboa, and I went up and made the turn and block-hopped behind her for three blocks. Just after she had crossed 33rd Avenue, she stopped in front of one of the stucco-fronted, pastel-colored apartment houses there, and looked both ways up and down the street; I was at the curb then, and she did not appear to notice me. She went into the foyer of the building.

I drove up to the corner and parked in front of somebody's driveway on the eastern side of 33rd. I waited two minutes, timing it by my watch, but she did not come back out. I left the car and crossed the street and walked slowly up to the building she had entered.

It was three stories, a dull green color, with a narrow circumscribed foyer and a thick glass-and-wood door barring admittance. A row of six mailboxes, above which were tiny white card strips enclosed in cellophane-covered brass plates, were on the right-hand wall. Each had a round ivory button just above it. I glanced at the names on each of the card strips, and the one for Apartment 4 read *Elaine and Lorraine Hanlon* in a neat, precise, feminine printing. I stepped out of the foyer and looked at the number in the rectangular lighted frame set into the stucco wall. Then I walked back to the car and got inside and tried to decide if I should wait around for a while, just in case, or get to the nearest phone as quickly as possible.

I was reaching for the ignition key, having settled on the phone, when the blonde came out of the entranceway and ran across the street.

I sat up a little straighter on the seat. She was a big girl, with long legs flashing bare and smooth under a short cotton coat and heavy breasts stretching the buttoned front of it. Her hair was the artificial color of champagne, worn long, streaming behind her in the wind like the mane of a thoroughbred at full gallop. She jerked open the door on a green Corvair Monza, but before she could get inside, the librarian came running into view with her arms extended outward and upward like a bird about to take flight. She had the shag coat and scarf off now, and I could see that her hair was cut short and close over her ears and that she was wearing a bulky white knit sweater over the gray tweed slacks. She looked almost pathetically thin—no hips, no breasts, a little girl who had never grown up and never would.

I had the window down now and I could hear her yelling something, but I could not understand the words. She ran over to the champagne blonde and caught her arm, but the blonde shrugged violently and the librarian stumbled backward a couple of steps, into the middle of the street. If there had been a car coming, it would have gotten her. The blonde slid inside the Corvair and slammed the door, and a moment later I could hear the starter grind viciously.

The librarian went back to the car and clawed at the window, but it was a futile and terrified scratching. Her face was turned toward me for a moment, and I could see that it was twisted with emotion; she might have been crying or she might have been mutely screaming.

The champagne blonde—almost assuredly Lorraine Hanlon—got the Corvair in gear and came away from the curb with the rear tires howling on the pavement, leaving the little girl standing there on the asphalt, small and desperate and alone. I had the Valiant started and moving along the street by then, and I pulled around Elaine Hanlon and went after her sister.

It was the same thing, perhaps, that a lot of men had been doing all of the librarian's life; and like them, I did not once look back.

13

Lorraine Hanlon drove with a kind of determined recklessness, leaning on the horn at cross streets and corners and to maneuver her way through traffic. She knew how to use the Corvair's standard transmission; I could hear the whine of the four-cylinder engine each time she geared down, and then again when she used a heavy foot before shifting up.

She went up to Geary Boulevard and turned east, heading downtown, and I stayed a block behind her, driving too fast so I could keep her in sight. I hoped a traffic cop did not tag her, because I had the feeling that she would try to outrun a red light or a siren—anything that denoted police authority. She was driving scared, running scared. It was not too difficult to figure why.

The librarian had been wrong, pathetically wrong. Her sister had not listened to her at all. When Elaine had told her, as she must have, that she had just been to see the detective involved in the Martinetti kidnapping, Lorraine had panicked. She was either too frightened or too deeply involved, or both, to want to give herself up to the police—and so she had run. I had no idea where she was running to, but it figured to be either to Lockridge's accomplice—if he had had one other than, perhaps, the blonde—or to where the boy was being held. Or a combination of both. The way she was driving, the way she had come flying out of that apartment building, said it had to be that way.

I drove grimly, both hands taut on the wheel, hunched forward a little. The Valiant had power steering, and it was loose and the car handled poorly; the model had never been built for maneuverability in the first place. It took all the concentration I was capable of to stay in a position where I could keep the green Corvair in sight, and that was just as well; it kept my mind off the gnawing ache in my stomach, the chilled numbness of my feet and hands which the car's heater did nothing to dispel.

The blonde made a sharp right turn, proceeding south, and beat the light into a left turn. I swore a little, coming up, and thought about running the red; but the cross traffic was heavy, and it would only have been inviting an accident. I reached the corner and peered down the slope of the street, and the blonde had gotten caught behind a beer truck at the light a couple of blocks down. I let breath spray between my teeth and took my hands off the wheel and worked some of the stiffness out of them, waiting for the green.

When it came, I closed the gap to a block again. The blonde brought the Corvair over into the left-hand lane as we neared the southbound Central Freeway approach. I got into the same lane and made the same light that she did, and I was six cars behind her climbing the banked and curving entrance ramp onto the freeway.

The midday traffic was heavy, and the Hanlon girl could not make any time at all on Central. She got around a couple of slow cars and a truck as we reached the Skyway and swung south onto Bayshore, opening the Corvair up, cutting across traffic with blind disregard until she had gotten into the outside lane. I edged over into the third of the four lanes and stayed there, moving out right or left when I encountered a car at a lesser speed than I was forced to drive.

The blonde remained in the outside lane until we neared the off-ramp at Army Street, and then she veered over, two lanes diagonally, narrowly missing a Volkswagen microbus. She made it into the exit lane. I went over there, too, and there was one car between us as we came down into the interchange on Army.

She turned right, onto Potrero Avenue, made three lights and missed a fourth. I was two blocks behind her. We passed San Francisco General Hospital, and when we reached Mariposa she swung right and went three blocks and made another right on De Haro. We were heading up onto Potrero Hill.

It was an industrial and low-rent housing area, with steep inclines and a lot of dead-end streets. I knew it well enough; I had had a girl friend who lived on Missouri Street at one time, and I had grown up in the Noe Valley District, not far away. I dropped back another block, giving her plenty of room; there was not much traffic now, and the risk of her spotting me was greater than it had been before.

At 23rd Street she took the Corvair left, crossed

Carolina Street and began climbing Wisconsin. I made the turn after her, just in time to see the green louvered rear deck of the Corvair swinging left onto Alaska Street.

I could feel the muscles in my arms and legs relax, and I worked saliva into my mouth. Alaska was a dead-end street, a single protracted block in length; Wisconsin was its only release street. I took the Valiant to the corner and stopped on the near side of it, in front of a small neighborhood grocery store. I looked up the steep incline to the leveled-off turning circle at its upper end. Lorraine Hanlon had pulled the Corvair to the curb off on the right of it, in front of an old shambling white house set well back behind a gray-white picket fence grown over with dry-looking rose bushes. A green tar-papered roof and the upper half of the facing wall of the house were all that was visible from where I was.

As I watched, the blonde got out of the Corvair and slammed the door and walked through a gate in the picket fence. She did not look anywhere except straight in front of her. A moment later she disappeared from my view.

I sat there for a short time, debating, and then I got out of the Valiant and began to walk up the hill. I did it slowly, because there was a tense pulsing in my lower belly. The wind blew strong and bitter cold up here; you could hear it moaning funereally in the now-leaden sky. From the southwest and Daly City, streamers of fog clutched at San Francisco like the tendrils of some obscene parasitic vine.

There were three houses on each side of the street going up, separated from one another by small brown yards and sagging fences of one kind or another. Shades and blinds and drapes were drawn against the hoary cheerlessness of the afternoon, and there was no sign of life anywhere. The only sound was the wind, and the empty, hollow slap of my shoes on the cracked sidewalk.

I reached the circle and paused there to drag breath into my lungs. There was a rasping ache in my chest now, from the climb. I had not thought about my lungs in two days, because I had had too many other things on my mind and I had gotten a good start on kicking the cigarette habit and there had been no recurrence of the coughing or wheezing. I thought about them now, briefly, and then I stopped thinking about them altogether. The skin beneath the bandage on my forehead began to itch; I wiped away cold sweat with the back of my hand and looked over at the white house.

It, and a smaller dwelling sided with brown wooden shingles, were angled like a pair of ears on the faceless head of the turning circle. A low wall constructed of weathered planks bisected the property and extended back as far as I could see. A glassed-in front porch covered the entire front of the house, and there was a set of steps inside a wooden block frame leading up to a screened-over front door. Split-bamboo blinds were lowered over the glass facing the street. Azalea and hydrangea shrubs, which would bloom wild in pink and white and lavender in the spring, filled the small yard between the picket fence and the house. Nothing moved anywhere on the grounds.

I got some of my breath back and went without hurrying to where the Corvair was pulled carelessly to the curb. I knelt down by the left rear tire and unscrewed the air valve, and then went around to the right rear tire and did the same thing. I straightened up again and looked at the house. Stillness.

I stepped away from the car, and I could hear the sibilance of escaping air from the tires. I walked directly to the brown-shingled cottage and went a little way down a weed-choked driveway paralleling the plank dividing wall, until I reached a point where I could see the rear grounds of the white house. Another plank wall extended the width of the property some forty feet in back of the dwelling, and then the terrain fell away sharply into a steep, rocky slope. It appeared to be unscalable.

I began to feel a little better about things. I pivoted and started back along the driveway, and a door opened and a fat woman in her late forties came out onto a podium-sized side porch. She had bright, curly orange hair that looked like carrot peelings pasted to her scalp. She wore a faded housedress and shedding blue mules.

I went over to the porch, and she came down a couple of steps and looked at me curiously, but without hostility. "Something you wanted?" she asked.

"Police business," I said.

"Yeah? What's going on?"

"Do you know who owns the house next door?" She shrugged. "Some realty company."

"Can you tell me who's renting it, then?"

"Man and his wife and their kid."

"What name?"

"Who knows?"

I pointed over at the green Corvair. "Was that the wife who just drove up a couple of minutes ago?"

"Didn't see her, but that's her car. She's got a couple of flat tires, looks like."

"Uh-huh," I said. "What about the husband?"

"What about him?"

"Can you describe him?"

"I only seen him once, from a distance," the woman said. "He looked like a million guys look, that's all."

"When was that one time you saw him?"

"Three days ago, I think it was."

"Tell me about the kid," I said. "A little boy?"

"Yeah."

"How old?"

"Nine or ten, maybe."

"Was he wearing a uniform?"

"What kind of uniform?"

"*Any* kind of uniform."

"No, he was wearing what kids always wear."

"Have you seen him in the past day or so?"

"No, not since him and his old man came that first day," the woman said. "You think I got nothing better to do than check who comes and goes around this neighborhood?"

"Don't you read the newspapers, lady?"

She made a snorting sound. "If I want rape and murder, I turn on the television."

"All right, then. As far as you know, the boy's still in the house."

"As far as I know."

"Anybody else?"

"The mother, I guess."

"Besides her."

"I couldn't say," the woman said. "Listen, what's going on? You going to arrest somebody?"

"Just routine, lady."

"Balls to that," the woman said knowingly. "I just hope there ain't going to be any shooting."

"Yeah," I said, and I left her there and went out of

the driveway and started down the hill. There was still no movement at the white house.

When I got to the corner, I turned into the small grocery store there. A clock on the rear wall, above a refrigerated case, said that it was almost three. Eberhardt had told me yesterday that he was working the four-to-midnight swing, and it was a safe assumption that he would have that tour all week; chances were good that he would still be home now.

I stepped up to a small check-out counter in front of a window looking out on Alaska Street. An old guy in a pair of red-and-gray suspenders was sitting on a stool, reading a pocketbook western. He looked up at me with tired eyes behind gold-rimmed spectacles. "Help you?"

"Have you got a phone here?"

"Pay phone?"

"Any kind of phone."

"Local call?"

"Police business," I said.

"Hell," the old guy said, "whyn't you say so?" He reached under the counter and brought out a telephone and put it down on the scarred surface. His eyes were not quite so tired now, watching me.

I moved around to where I could look through the window. The Corvair was visible from there, and the gate in the gray-white picket fence. I dialed Eberhardt's home number, and he answered on the third ring with typical cordiality: "Yeah, what is it?"

"Plenty, Eb," I said, and I gave it to him fast and sketched out. He did not interrupt. When I was finished, he said, "You think this Hanlon girl is in there alone with the kid?"

"It looks that way, but I can't be certain."

"Where are you now?"

"A little grocery store at the bottom of the hill."

"Can you see the house from there?"

"Yeah."

"You're sure she can't get out through the rear?"

"Not down that slope, she can't."

"And you disabled her car?"

"Two flat rear tires."

"Okay," Eberhardt said. "I'll have a couple of plainclothesmen there in fifteen minutes, and squad cars on stand-by in the area."

"Are you coming yourself?"

"Twenty minutes from here."

"No sirens, Eb."

"Hell no," he said, and rang off.

I gave the phone back to the old guy. He was sitting there with his mouth hinged open. "Goddamn," he said. "God-*damn!*"

I stood at the window and stared up the hill and nothing happened. The old guy kept looking at me with his eyes bright and excited behind the spectacles, and it began to make me nervous. I went outside and leaned against the building, head bowed against the sting of the wind.

Sixteen minutes had passed when the unmarked black Ford sedan came hurtling up Wisconsin, slowed midway in the block, and pulled smoothly and silently to the curb behind Erika's Valiant. Four men in dark suits got out and came over in front of the grocery. I knew one of them slightly—an inspector named Gilette.

He touched my shoulder in greeting and said, "Anything happen since you called the lieutenant?"

"Nothing, Ray."

He moved to where he could look up the hill. "Which house is it?" he asked me.

"The big white one at the end."

"Okay."

"What now?" one of the other inspectors said. He was young and sandy-haired and grim-jawed.

"We wait for the lieutenant," Gilette told him.

Eberhardt arrived three minutes later. I was staring down Wisconsin, and I saw his four-year-old Dodge make the turn off 23rd Street and pass a patrol car that had pulled up there in the event it was needed. He took the Dodge in behind the unmarked sedan and got out and walked over to us with his long legs moving in wide, hard strides.

Eberhardt seemed to have been fashioned of an odd contrast of sharp angles and smooth blunt planes. He had a high, squarely intelligent forehead, a slender bifurcated nose, a perfectly even mouth, a sharply V-pointed chin. His upper torso was thick and blocky, but he had those long legs and the long-fingered angular hands of a musician. His hair, a light brown color made to seem dusty by a salting of gray, was wavy on the sides and straight on top. He was wearing a loose topcoat over a perennial off-the-rack blue suit that was too tight in the shoulders and too baggy in the legs. In a corner of his mouth was another perennial fixture: a short-stemmed, flame-scarred black briar pipe, cold and empty now.

He nodded to me and said grimly, "She still up there?"

"Uh-huh," I said.

Gilette took him to the corner and pointed out the house. "Sheffield and I will go up on either side if you want it that way, Lieutenant."

"Yeah," Eberhardt said. He looked at the sandy-haired cop. "Go ahead, Sheff, but take it nice and slow."

"Right."

I watched Sheffield cross the street and start up the hill on the other side. Eberhardt let him get forty yards along, and then said to Gilette, "Go, Ray."

Gilette moved out on this side like a guy looking for a particular house in an unfamiliar neighborhood. Eberhardt said to the other two inspectors, "When they get up there and in position, the three of us will move. Dan, around to the back door. Jack, you and I right up the stairs in front."

They nodded in wordless understanding, and the four of us stood there and watched Gilette and Sheffield climbing the hill. There should have been some tension in the cold air, but I could not feel it; maybe it was because the whole thing was out of my hands now, and there was no more pressure.

Sheffield had reached the circle and was starting around the Corvair, and Gilette was nearing the point where the street leveled off, when the blonde suddenly came out of the house holding tightly onto the arm of a small boy.

I stiffened, leaning across Eberhardt's shoulder, and I could see that the boy was wearing dungarees and a lightweight jacket. He appeared to be unafraid. And then he and Lorraine Hanlon came through the gate in the picket fence and she saw Gilette and Sheffield hurriedly converging on her with their coats thrown back now and their hands resting on the butts of the service revolvers holstered at their belts.

She came to a complete standstill there on the sidewalk. She did not try to run; she made no move at all.

She just stood there like a piece of sculpture, holding on to Gary Martinetti's arm, until Sheffield reached her and took her hand away.

Eberhardt and the other two inspectors ran up to the top of the hill and through the gate and scattered across the yard. Gilette and Sheffield pulled the blonde and the boy out of the way. Eberhardt kicked open the front door, and he and the cop called Jack went into the house with drawn guns. But by the time I made it up to the circle they had reappeared again, revolvers holstered, to announce that the premises were otherwise empty.

That's all there was to it.

14

Eberhardt said, "We'll talk to the boy first."

We were in the house now, in a narrow and musty-smelling hallway just off the kitchen. In the living room, Sheffield and the inspector named Dan were standing watch over Lorraine Hanlon; the third inspector, Jack, was with Gary Martinetti in a rear bedroom, and Ray Gilette was making a systematic search of the house.

I said, "Whatever you think, Eb."

We went down the hallway and into the bedroom. The boy was sitting on the edge of a rumpled iron-frame double bed, his hands folded quietly in his lap. He was a nice-looking kid: lean, agile, in the well-fitting dungarees and jacket, with big soft colt-brown eyes and tousled black hair. He looked up as we came in and smiled at us; we had introduced ourselves to him when we'd first brought him inside.

I looked around the bedroom. The only furniture

in there, in addition to the bed, was an unvarnished wooden dresser and a straight-backed chair pushed under a small table at one wall. The table held a couple of empty plates and a tumbler that looked as if it had contained milk at one time, a toy battleship that had been neatly put together from a model set, the plastic components of a second battleship only just begun, and some hardbound children's adventure books stacked in a neat pile on one end. The room's single window was fastened down on this side and shuttered across the outside, with an outside latch. A door on the left side of the room opened into a small blue-tile bathroom; there was no window in there that I could see.

Eberhardt said to Gary, "How you feeling, son? All right?"

"Oh, sure. I'm fine, sir."

That kind of politeness went a long way with Eberhardt. He sat down on the bed and put his arm around the boy's narrow shoulders. "We'll be taking you home pretty soon. I guess you're kind of anxious to see your mom and dad."

"Yes, *sir!*"

"But you won't mind answering a couple of questions for us first, will you?"

"No, sir."

"That's fine," Eberhardt said. "Now the first thing—I want to know if you were hurt in any way. Slapped, shoved, anything like that."

"No, Miss Frye was pretty nice to me," Gary said.

"Miss Frye, huh?"

"Yes, sir."

"The blond girl out front?"

"Uh-huh."

"What about the man? What was his name?"

"You mean the man who came for me at Sandhurst?"

"That's the one."

"He said for me to call him Kenneth."

Lockridge's first name had been Paul. Eberhardt apparently knew that as well, because he nodded to himself in his dour way. I had the idea that he had briefed himself thoroughly on the details of the kidnapping and murder of Lockridge—not so much because I was involved in it, but more because he was a good cop who liked to keep fully informed on matters which fell, no matter how peripherally, under his jurisdiction.

He said, "And this Kenneth was nice to you too, was he?"

"Yes, sir, I guess he was," Gary answered.

"Did he tell you why you were being taken out of school?"

"He said my dad wanted him to."

"Where did you go after you left Sandhurst?"

"We stopped at a service station and Kenneth gave me a bag with these clothes I'm wearing now inside, and said I was to change out of my uniform."

"And then what?"

"We drove up here in Kenneth's car."

"You mean here to this house?"

"Uh-huh."

"Was Miss Frye here when you arrived?"

"Yes, sir," Gary said. "Kenneth introduced me to her, and then he brought me into this room and showed me the Tom Swift books there—some that I haven't read before—and the models and said I was going to be staying here for a couple of days."

"Did you ask him why?"

"Sure," the boy said. "He just laughed and told me it was a big secret."

"What did you say to that?"

"Well, that I thought something pretty funny was going on. And he said oh, you do? and I said yes, maybe you better take me home now. He just laughed again and locked me up in here so I couldn't get out at all."

"Were you afraid?"

"Well, a little, I guess."

"Did you know what was happening?"

"Sure," the boy said matter-of-factly. "I was being kidnapped. I knew for sure when he took me out a little while later to talk to my dad on the phone, after Miss Frye had gone out shopping."

Eberhardt said, "Did you see Kenneth again after that first day?"

"Uh-huh. He came the next morning, and I could hear him and Miss Frye yelling at each other out in the living room."

"What were they yelling about?"

"Miss Frye said she didn't want anything to do with a kidnapping and Kenneth said it was too late now, she already had something to do with it, and Miss Frye started to cry and Kenneth said for her not to worry because it would all be over tonight—that night, I mean—and they could go back East and live it up."

"Did Kenneth come and talk to you personally?"

"For a little while, he did."

"What did he say?"

"He told me to be good and stay quiet, and I could go home that night."

"Did you do what he said?"

"Yes, sir. I wanted to go home."

"But Kenneth didn't come back, did he?"

"No, sir, he didn't. Did you catch him?"

"Not exactly," Eberhardt said. He chewed noiselessly on the stem of his pipe. "Did Miss Frye feed you regularly?"

"Nothing but a lot of sandwiches," Gary said. "I'm awful tired of sandwiches."

"And did she come talk to you?" Eberhardt asked. "Did she let you out of here at all?"

"She didn't let me out," Gary said. "I guess 'cause she was afraid I'd try to run or something if she did. There's two doors into the bathroom, and she'd lock this one and put some milk and sandwiches in there and then unlock it again so I could get the stuff."

"Tell me what happened yesterday, Gary."

"Nothing much. Miss Frye went around slamming things and I could hear her walking up and down. Then she went out and came back and after that she was pretty quiet. But I could hear her bawling once when I went over to the door to listen."

"Did she leave you alone last night?"

"No," Gary said, "but she left awful early this morning. I heard the front door slam, and then it got quiet the way it does when nobody's around, so I knew she'd gone away. I tried yelling for a while, but I didn't think anybody could hear me, so I quit that. Then I thought about breaking the window, but those shutters are latched on the outside; you can see it if you look hard—the latch, I mean. I just sat here and waited." He looked down at the sterile whiteness of the cheap new tennis shoes on his small feet, and as if ashamed he said, "I cried once, too—but only for a little while."

"What did Miss Frye say to you when she came this afternoon?" Eberhardt asked gently.

"She didn't say anything right away. I heard her come into the house and pace around for a while and rattle some glasses and stuff in the kitchen. Then she came and told me she was going to see that I got home because it was the only thing for her to do. Then she unlocked the door and got hold of my arm and took me outside, and that's when you and the other officers came and rescued me."

Eberhardt patted the boy's head and got up on his feet. "You're a brave boy, Gary," he said. "You stay with Inspector Nelson over there for a few minutes while I talk to Miss Frye, and then we'll see that you get right home. Okay?"

"Yes, sir," the boy said, and smiled up at us. It was an infectious smile, and we were both grinning as we went out.

In the hallway, I said, "Some kid, huh, Eb?"

"Yeah," Eberhardt said. "That's a fact, all right."

We went down the hall to the living room.

15

It was dark in there, with only a single tassel-shaded floor lamp on one side of the room casting pale light over the drab interior. The furniture was old and tired and dusty; a faded crocheted afghan covered the backrest of an overstuffed velveteen couch, and there were yellow-tinged antimacassars on the arms of two matching chairs.

In the exact center of the couch, Lorraine Hanlon sat with her knees pressed tightly together, her hands twisted in a large handkerchief. The long blond hair seemed damp and lifeless and painfully artificial in the dimness, and her coral-colored lips were starkly contrasted to the pinched whiteness of a softly round face. She would have been, in other circumstances, attractive in a faintly brassy, too-voluptuous way; hers was the kind of prettiness that would fade rapidly after thirty-five and the inevitable advent of poundage in all the wrong places.

Sheffield and the inspector named Dan were sitting quietly in the two overstuffed chairs, angled to face the couch. I stayed behind them, out of the way, and Eberhardt walked over and stood in front of the girl. She lifted her head to look at him, and there was a kind of dull fear in her violet-shadowed eyes. She had said nothing at all that I knew of since she had been taken into custody, but I had the feeling that she would not be uncooperative. The fear was too obviously strong in her.

Eberhardt said, "You've been put under arrest, Miss Hanlon, and it's my duty to advise you of your personal rights." He went on to do that, and concluded with, "Do you understand all of your rights as I've outlined them?"

In a small voice that was reminiscent of the librarian's, she said, "Yes, I understand."

"Are you willing, then, to answer questions without the presence of counsel?"

She sighed softly and nodded.

"All right, Miss Hanlon," Eberhardt said. He rested one hip against the curved arm of the couch, and looked over at Sheffield; Sheffield had a note pad and a pencil poised on his right knee. "Suppose you tell us your story."

"Where should I start?" dully, resignedly.

"Start with Kenneth," Eberhardt said. "Or maybe you knew him as Paul Lockridge."

"Yes," Lorraine said, "Paul Lockridge." There was bitterness mingled with the wooden resignation now —bitterness and something else, too, an emotion perhaps far more basic.

"How long did you know him?"

"About three weeks," she said. "I met him one night in the Copper Penny, on Union Street. We had some drinks and he asked me out and I accepted. He was a very . . . very smooth guy. Do you know?"

"Yeah. What did he tell you about himself?"

"Not very much. He said he was from Cleveland or someplace like that in the Midwest, and that he was in San Francisco on business."

"What kind of business?"

"He never told me."

"Didn't you ask him?"

"Sure, but he just made some joke about it being one of those things the world wasn't quite ready for, and he'd got in on the ground floor. Or something like that."

"And that's all he confided in you?"

"About himself, yes," Lorraine said. "I thought it was a little funny, you know? because he seemed like the kind of guy who would talk about himself a lot, but he always changed the subject when I asked him. He was . . . sort of mysterious and exciting. Do you know?"

Eberhardt nodded sourly and said, "You dated him regularly the past three weeks, is that right?"

"Yes."

"Where did he live?"

"The Jack Tar Hotel."

Eberhardt glanced briefly in my direction, and we were both thinking the same thing: the Jack Tar was a huge downtown hotel, catering to visiting businessmen, and the flow through there was heavy and constant. There was nothing particularly memorable about Lockridge, from the photo I had seen in the paper, and he would have blended perfectly, anonymously, into the milieu—just another average face in a thousand average faces a week. That seemed to explain why there had been no response as yet to the news media's plea for assistance; he had apparently checked out of the Tar immediately prior to driving up into the San Bruno hills to the ransom drop, which also explained the suitcase he had had in the rented car. Registration cards are filed away quickly in a place like the Jack Tar, and if he had not used his name often, there was no reason why any of the clerks or bellboys would have remembered it.

Eberhardt said, "Where did you go when you went out with Lockridge?"

"Nightclubs, mostly. North Beach and over to Jack London Square in Oakland. Like that."

"He had plenty of money, then."

"He seemed to have."

"Did you always go alone, just the two of you?"

"Yes."

"Did he have any friends in the Bay Area that you know about?"

"I don't think so."

"He never mentioned anyone?"

"Well," Lorraine said slowly, "just this cousin he said lived down the Peninsula."

"What was this cousin's name?"

"He didn't say, but I think he must have been referring to what he was going to do—the kidnapping, I mean. I don't think there really was a cousin." A shudder passed through her, and she twisted the handkerchief into a tight rope between her trembling hands. Her eyes roamed Eberhardt's face imploringly. "You've got to believe one thing: I didn't know Paul was going to kidnap that little boy until after he'd already done it. I swear to God I didn't; I wouldn't have gotten mixed up in it if I had."

Eberhardt tapped the stem of his pipe against his

front teeth and said nothing for a long moment. Then: "What was his story to you in the beginning?"

"He . . . he said that this cousin of his had a little boy, and Paul was going to take care of him for a couple of days while the cousin went somewhere on a trip. But he said the boy was kind of a problem child and had this big imagination, and he was being punished on account of some kid's trick he'd pulled. He was supposed to be locked up in his room."

"And you believed all that?"

She looked at her quaking hands. "I . . . I wanted to believe him. He said we'd go away together, back East someplace. He said he was coming into a lot of money very soon."

"Uh-huh," Eberhardt said.

"It's the truth, I swear it. He asked me if I would watch over the boy for a couple of days while he attended to some business, and just not to pay attention to what the boy said. He told me to go ahead and quit my job—I worked for this accounting firm as a secretary—and we'd leave as soon as the boy went home to the cousin. It seemed all right, it really did."

"Who rented this house? Lockridge?"

"Yes, by telephone I think he said. But I didn't even know about this place until Paul told me the night before he brought the boy."

"Didn't you think it was kind of odd? That he had rented a house when he was getting ready to leave the Bay Area? That he was living in a hotel instead of here if he'd had it all along?"

"Yes, a little. But I . . . liked Paul. I didn't want anything to be wrong, don't you see?"

"When did you decide something *was* wrong?"

"After he brought the boy here," Lorraine said, "and locked him up in the bedroom so fast."

"But you didn't say anything to him then."

"No." She kept on twisting the handkerchief. "I did a lot of thinking that night, and I decided that maybe . . . maybe Paul had kidnapped the boy."

"Why didn't you call the authorities right then?"

"I wasn't sure, that's why. I wanted to ask Paul. But when I called the hotel, he wasn't there. So I . . . I just waited."

"And when he came the next day, what did you do?"

"I told him what I suspected."

"Did he deny it?"

"At first he did, but then he just shrugged and admitted it. He said there was a lot of money involved, and some other considerations too, but that there were no risks and I shouldn't worry." She laughed humorlessly, bitterly. "No risks—and now he's dead."

Eberhardt said, "So you went along with him."

"What could I do? I was already involved, wasn't I? And he kept saying nothing could go wrong. I couldn't . . . I couldn't just sit down and call the police. Besides, I . . . oh, damn it, I loved him. I loved Paul Lockridge! I wanted to be with him, to live the way he said we would live, to have the things I've never had before. Do you see, do you know?"

It was very quiet. The only sound was Sheffield's pencil moving across the rough paper of the note pad. I felt a little sorry for Lorraine Hanlon, for all the Lorraine Hanlons of the world. They were early-blossoming flesh —nature's compensation for insipid intelligence ofttimes—

and sensuality in lieu of rationality was their way. They measured happiness in material possessions and hedonistic accomplishments, and they invariably believed their bodies before they listened to their minds. They were ripe prey, standard fodder, for the appetites and manipulations of men like Paul Lockridge. Lorraine Hanlon was a pawn, the same way her little librarian sister was a pawn—on different sides of the board, perhaps, but still a pawn, always a pawn, and life sacrifices its pawns for the same reasons a chess player sacrifices his: to protect and maintain the stronger and more powerful ones, the rooks and the knights, the king and the queen.

Eberhardt broke the protracted stillness, finally, by asking quietly, "Lockridge was suppose to come for you the night of the ransom delivery, wasn't he?"

"Yes," Lorraine answered dolorously. "He said it would be late, after eleven. Then we would take the boy down the Peninsula and let him off somewhere and just keep on driving. We would go to Las Vegas first . . ." Her eyes were dry, but there was pain in them that was evident even from where I was; it was the pain of shattered hopes and a future filled with grayness. "But he didn't come. I waited up until three o'clock, and then I went to bed but I didn't sleep at all."

"What did you think had happened?"

"I thought . . . I thought he'd just gone off without me. That he'd gotten the money and left me to handle the boy."

"But you weren't sure, and you did nothing."

"That's right. I waited all through the next day, yesterday, and finally I couldn't take any more of this house and I went out to buy a newspaper. And I saw . . . saw Paul's photo and that he was dead . . ."

Eberhardt said, "Why didn't you let the boy go last night, after you came back?"

"I was afraid," she said. "I thought you—the police—might think I had something to do with Paul's murder. I was confused and . . . and sick over his death. I told you, I loved him."

"What decided you today?"

"I had to have somebody to talk to, some company; I couldn't stay in this house another minute. I went to where I've been living with my sister. She could tell something was wrong, and she had recognized Paul's picture from the one time he had come there to pick me up on a date; she went to talk to a detective"—her eyes flicked over to me, quickly, and then fastened again on the handkerchief she was still knotting between her fingers—"and when she came back and told me what she'd done and tried to get me to turn myself in, I just . . . I panicked. The only thing I could think to do was get back here and take the boy someplace and release him, and that way I would be safe."

"What were you going to do then?"

"Run away, I guess, I don't know where. Just run away. I . . . oh God, oh God!" She put her face in her hands and the tears came then, swift and silent, and her body oscillated heavily, as if she were caught between two powerful and unresisting magnets.

Eberhardt stood and looked at me and shook his head in a kind of sadly cynical way. Then he turned and went over to Sheffield and said softly, "Take her down to the Hall, Sheff, you and Dan. It's time the boy's parents were notified that he's all right; after that, we'll be taking him home."

Eberhardt and I went into the cluttered, ancientapplianced kitchen. Just as we did, Ray Gilette came in through the back door. He said, "I went over everything, inside and out, Lieutenant. No weapons and no suitcase filled with money. A flat zero."

Eberhardt nodded. He looked over at a wall phone above a plastic-topped dinette littered with coffee cups and empty glasses and an ashtray overflowing with coral-tipped cigarette butts. "You want to make the call?" he asked me. "You're the fair-haired boy."

"I'd like that, Eb," I said.

"Go ahead, then."

I went over to the phone and dialed Martinetti's number from memory. He answered personally on the first ring. I told him in clear, fast words that his son had been found, that Gary was fine and safe, that he would be brought home in just a little while. I listened to a giant explosion of breath, to humbly murmured words, "Thank God, thank God." I told him the rest of it then, touching high points for him, and I had just finished when I heard Karyn Martinetti's voice demanding shrilly, plaintively, in the background, "What is it, Lou, what is it?"—and Martinetti's answer, "Gary's been found, he's safe, he's coming home," and her low cry of relief, joy, and then the sound of weeping.

There were some confused moments then, and I heard other voices in the background—Proxmire's, what seemed like Donleavy's. I could picture the scene in Martinetti's study or wherever he was talking from: the deep sighs of total relief, the wan and tired smiles, the weakness of limbs that comes with the sudden and complete collapse of tension. I could almost feel the elation, the relief, emanating over the wire; the two emotions were strong inside me as well as I sat there holding the phone and listening.

Finally Martinetti said, "Are you still there? We've got a little bit of a carnival atmosphere here right now."

"It's nice to hear," I said.

He laughed softly, a little numbly. "I just don't know what to say."

"You don't need to say anything, Mr. Martinetti," I told him. "I think I understand how you feel."

"Will you be bringing Gary home yourself?"

"I'll be coming along, yes."

"Good. That's good."

"We should be there within the hour."

"This girl, this accomplice of Lockridge's," he said. "Has she told you anything about his death, or about the money?"

"A few things, but nothing vital. We'll tell you about it when we get down there."

"All right." He paused to listen to a voice near him, and then said, "Mr. Donleavy wants to talk to you."

"Okay."

Donleavy's voice came on the line. "Nice work," he said, and he sounded genuinely complimentary, genuinely pleased. "I was listening over Mr. Martinetti's shoulder."

"Thanks, Donleavy."

"Listen, who's in charge up there?"

"Lieutenant Eberhardt."

"Yeah, I know him a little," Donleavy said. "He's a good man. Can you put him on?"

"Sure."

Eberhardt was leaning on the drainboard, tamping tobacco from a cracked leather pouch into his pipe. I motioned to him and he came over and took the phone and

talked to Donleavy for a while. Eb gave him a fast run-
down of what we had learned in talking to the boy and to
Lorraine Hanlon; from his end of the remainder of the
conversation I gathered that Donleavy was sending Reese
up to San Francisco to talk to Lorraine at the Hall, and
that he was staying at Martinetti's to wait for our arrival.

Eberhardt rang off eventually and got out a butane
pipe lighter and put flame to the black briar bowl. When
he had it drawing to his satisfaction, he said, "Come on,
hot shot. Let's go give a little boy back to his family."

16

It was almost five-thirty when I turned Erika's Valiant onto Tamarack Drive in Hillsborough. There were a couple of cars pulled up outside number 416—a dark brown Ford and a black Plymouth—and I supposed they belonged to Donleavy and maybe some other one of the District Attorney's people. I parked behind the Plymouth on the cool, quiet street; a thin early-evening breeze sent oak and eucalyptus leaves skipping among the deepening shadows cast by the surrounding trees.

Gary had the rear door open almost before I had brought the Valiant to a complete stop. He ran up to the wooden footbridge and across it and swung open the gate. Eberhardt and I got out and watched him running up the gravel path with his legs and arms pumping like a well-coached sprinter. The front door opened before he got fifty feet, and Karyn Martinetti—slender and very young-looking in a pale yellow cotton dress—came flying out with her arms stretched wide, shouting, "Gary, Gary, Gary!" and enclosed him in her grasp and swung him around and clung to him with a possessiveness that was almost feral in its intensity. Her face was sheened with tears, free of cosmetics, and she looked radiant now that her son was safe again in her arms.

"Oh, honey, Gary, are you all right, did they hurt you, how do you feel, honey?" she crooned at him.

He hugged her, and then patted her brushed blond hair in a kind of manly tolerance for the histrionics of women. "Sure, Mom," he said, "I'm okay. You don't have to worry any more."

She made half-laughing, half-crying sounds and kept on holding him very close to her breast. I looked beyond them and saw that Martinetti—with Proxmire at his heels—had come outside now; both of them wore rumpled slacks and old sweaters and weary smiles. They hunkered down, one on either side of the woman and the boy, and Martinetti clasped his son's face between his hands and kissed his forehead. Proxmire looked as if he wanted to do the same thing, but he just squatted there with an odd sadness to the cast of his face and his eyes shining a little as he looked at Gary. I thought: He's really fond of that boy, you can't fake a look like that.

Beside me, Eberhardt said softly, "This is kind of a nice thing to see, but somehow it makes you uncomfortable to watch it."

"Yeah," I said. "I know what you mean, Eb."

We stood quietly out of the way and let them have their reunion in some privacy. I noticed that Donleavy stood framed in the doorway, in blue dacron today, allowing the Martinettis and Proxmire the same privilege; he looked typically sad and sleepy. Eberhardt shuffled his feet around and began to fill his pipe with quick, nervous gestures. I thought his discomfiture was partially due to the poignancy he was witnessing, and partially because he felt no more at home in a milieu like Hillsborough than I did.

Martinetti straightened up after a time and walked over to where Eberhardt and I were standing. The change in him, now that his son had been found and returned home, was considerable; but the deep fissures in the hewn granite were still visible, and his eyes remained sunken even though there was life in them again—some of the strength and power of the man. The draining tension, the total lack of sleep, the fear and the worry, had left marks which would not heal in a single day or a single week. It would be some time yet before the haunted, skeletal look of him was completely gone, before the chiseled features were smooth and hard and clear of the corpselike grayness which still faintly tinged them.

He reached for my hand and shook it warmly and thanked me mutely with his eyes. Then he looked at Eb and said, "Is this Lieutenant Eberhardt?"

I said, "Yes, it is," and made simple introductions.

"I'd like to shake your hand, too, Lieutenant," Martinetti said, and they did that solemnly. He smiled with infinite weariness. "Come into the house. We'll have a celebratory drink. God, I could use a drink just now."

Eberhardt said he could use one, too, and that was unusual, because he did not like to take anything alcoholic when he was on duty; he was old-fashioned, or perhaps the word is sensible, that way. His agreeableness to the offer told me just how uncomfortable he was.

We followed Martinetti along the path. His wife was taking Gary into the house now, her arm tight around his shoulders, holding him hard against her side; she was not about to let go of him just yet. Proxmire followed them and then stopped at the door and hovered there nervously; when Martinetti went in and Eberhardt followed him, Proxmire took my arm and drew me aside.

"Listen," he said earnestly, "I want to apologize for this morning."

There was genuine contrition on the deeply hollowed surface of his face, in the tired and pouched depths of his eyes. I said, "You were under a heavy strain, Proxmire, I can understand that."

"Yes, but I had no call to come down on you that way. I . . . feel like a complete ass."

"We all feel like asses now and then," I said. "Let's just forget about it, why don't we?"

"No hard feelings?"

"No," I said, "no hard feelings."

"You're a generous man," Proxmire said, and gave me his hand. I took it, and he smiled, and we stepped into the house.

The others were in the living room, and we went in there. Donleavy was standing over by the draped window with Eberhardt, talking softly to him. Karyn Martinetti had been sitting on the couch; she got to her feet when she saw me and threw her arms around my neck without shame and kissed me hard on the cheek. Her hair was very soft and smelled of violets in a pleasantly vague sort of way.

She whispered, "Thank you," and stepped back, smiling, her eyes still wet. Then she turned back to the couch and sat down with her arm around Gary's shoulders.

Martinetti and the maid, Cassy, entered from the opposite end of the living room. She was carrying a silver tray with some brandy snifters and a full decanter and a large glass of Cola on it; a wide smile on her thin mouth made her seem brighter, prettier, than I remembered her. There was no one else present that I could see, and I thought that that was just as well. I would not have trusted my manners if Channing had been there, not after that phone call this morning.

Martinetti poured us all a drink from the decanter and gave the glass of Cola to Gary, and we drank a toast. I put mine back neat, and saw that Donleavy and Eberhardt had done the same thing. Donleavy came over to where I was. "I've got something to show you and Eberhardt," he said. "But not in here."

"All right."

He nodded and said to Martinetti, "You'll excuse us, won't you? We've got some things to talk over."

"Of course."

"We'll use your study, if that's all right."

"Yes, certainly."

Donleavy went out into the entrance hall and down the side hallway and through the ornately carved doors into the study. Eberhardt and I followed him. Donleavy shut the door and went over to the desk and switched on the lamp there. Then he took a small rectangular object from the pocket of his suit jacket and laid it carefully in the pool of illumination on the polished surface.

It was made of black styrene plastic, about the size of a small wooden matchbox. On the near side was a tiny on-and-off slide switch. There was a rubber grommet in one end, with four thin spidery wires—one red, one white, one green, one blue—protruding from it, about six inches each in length; at the end of each wire was a tooth-type alligator clip with a tiny rubber boot covering it as a preventive against shorting.

Donleavy said, "I guess you know what that is."

"Phone bug," Eberhardt said sourly.

I asked, "Where'd you find it?"

"I didn't find it myself," Donleavy said a little ruefully. "Reese found it. Reese is an eager-beaver, and he gets a lot of ideas. Every now and then, one of them pays off—like this one." Donleavy reached out and tapped the telephone on the desk with the blunt tip of his forefinger. "He opened up the base of this unit here, about a half-hour before you called, and there it was."

I looked at the bug. It was a simple package, nothing more than a miniature frequency-modulation transmitter. Its wires would have been attached, by way of the tooth clips, to the four leads coming into the phone; either an incoming or outgoing call would have activated it and transmitted an FM signal to a monitor somewhere in the immediate area. Judging from the size of the package, the monitor would have to have been put up within approximately a half-block radius. With a bug like that you could pick up conversations through a standard FM radio, tuned to a place on the dial which was not licensed for local broadcasting; somebody sitting in a car, for example, could monitor calls on the automobile's radio. Or if he was afraid of the conspicuousness of a lengthy plant, all he would have to have done would be to run a patch cord between the input jack on a cassette tape recorder and the earphone jack on a portable radio, and then secrete both units in any one of a hundred places in the vicinity. The phone conversations would be fed directly from the opened line through the radio and into the recorder, ready for him to replay when he retrieved the equipment.

Donleavy said, "We've got a couple of men out combing the area now, but I don't expect them to find anything. Not with a bug like this one."

"This complicates hell out of things, doesn't it?" I said slowly.

"Yeah, and I don't like it one goddamn bit." Donleavy went over and sat down on the couch with a ponderousness that reminded me of Oliver Hardy. He crossed his ankles and folded his hands on top of his paunch, and he looked very soft sitting there that way. He was about as soft as petrified wood. "There's no way of telling how long that thing was in the phone; could have been planted before the kidnapping or after it. If we knew which one, it would help."

"Assuming that it has something to do with the snatch in the first place," Eberhardt said morosely.

"Nuts to coincidences," Donleavy said.

I asked, "Does Martinetti have any ideas?"

"Well, to begin with, he tells me that he had a party here two nights before the boy was taken from Sandhurst, one of those catered deals out on the terrace with about sixty or seventy people milling around. Any one of them could have planted the bug; it would take about three minutes, and the only requirements, a pocket screwdriver and maybe a little knowledge of electronics."

"What about after the snatch?"

"It's possible. Martinetti and Channing were down to Martinetti's office in Redwood City, going over his books most of the night of the kidnapping; Mrs. Martinetti went to bed early, so did the maid, and Proxmire went home." He waved a hand toward the draped windows behind the desk. "The catches on those windows could be slipped with a penknife; anybody could have come in here that night and bugged the phone and gotten away in less than ten minutes with no trouble at all."

"If it happened that way," I said, "whoever it was had to know there *was* a kidnapping—that the boy had been abducted from the military academy that day."

"Yeah."

"In addition to the headmaster at Sandhurst, the only ones who knew that were myself, Channing and Proxmire and the maid and the Martinettis."

"Well, the headmaster—Young—has an unimpeachable reputation and a bank account in six figures," Donleavy said. "He seems to be in the clear."

"Which puts emphasis on the theory that one of the people here engineered a hijacking of the ransom money," I said. "But all of them were right in this house at the time Lockridge and I were attacked up in the hills."

"One of them could have had an accomplice," Eberhardt suggested.

"There are too damned many accomplices in this thing," Donleavy said. "But I'll admit it's a possibility."

I said, "Are you eliminating the theory of Lockridge having any partner except the Hanlon girl—at least as far as his murder is concerned?"

"I think we can, yeah, from what the girl told you. We also got a report on Lockridge from the Cleveland police first thing this morning, and as far as they could find out, he was strictly a loner."

"What was his background?" Eberhardt asked.

Donleavy made a distasteful noise with his lips. "Rogue cop," he said. "He was thrown off the Louisville police force about twelve years ago, for taking bribes from a string of horse parlors. He moved up to Cleveland and tried to get on with some security outfits, but with his past, they wouldn't touch him. He'd never been in trouble in the Cleveland area, and the police there don't have anything on him. But it's rumored that he had some underworld connections here and there, among others, and that he paid the rent hustling angles and information."

"Kidnapping doesn't fit that kind of guy too well," Eberhardt said. "But I guess three hundred thousand dollars is plenty of temptation for any man to gamble for."

We let silence build for a few moments, thinking our own thoughts. An idea occurred to me, and I said, "Listen, suppose Lockridge *did* have a partner after all, a kind of silent partner, somebody who knew him for one reason or another and who also knew the Martinettis. Suppose this silent partner got in touch with Lockridge with the kidnap scheme and brought him out here to California to do the job. Hell, somebody had to tip Lockridge to the situation; according to the Hanlon girl, he'd only been out here for three weeks, and he was talking about 'a business deal' from the beginning. It doesn't figure that he would come all the way from Cleveland to pull a snatch without having a victim in mind; and living back there, how would he know who to pick in California?"

"Why wouldn't the silent partner do the job himself?" Eberhardt asked, making argument.

"Maybe because the boy knew him by sight," I answered. "It would have been a risky proposition, pulling it off himself if he was known to any member of the family."

"Okay, you've got a good point," Donleavy said. "It would explain the kidnap note on Martinetti's stationery adequately enough, from what he tells me about his office layout—and it would also explain something else that's been bothering me: how Lockridge knew the San

Bruno hills well enough, being from out of state, to use that dirt road as a ransom drop. Sure, he could have driven around looking for a likely place, but since he was staying in San Francisco, why would he pick something so far south? There are other isolated areas, closer ones, that he might have chosen." He uncrossed his ankles and crossed them the other way. "But what it *doesn't* explain is the bug."

"It could if the bug is nothing more than a red herring to hamper an investigation. The partner and Lockridge could have cooked that up figuring you would examine every possibility."

"That makes them out to be master criminals," Eberhardt said in his dour way. "Master criminals are fine for those pulp magazines of yours, but they're a plain crock in real life and you know it."

Donleavy's eyes were speculative. "Now that I think of it, I can figure an explanation for the tap myself. This silent partner, assuming there is one, would likely have wanted as little contact with Lockridge as possible once Lockridge reached California—for obvious reasons. If he distrusted him, he could have used the bug to make sure Lockridge kept up his end of the deal."

"Fine," Eberhardt said, "but why would he bring Lockridge in in the first place if he distrusted him? And why, for Christ's sake, would this silent partner kill Lockridge up at the drop site? Why wouldn't he just wait until the pickup had been made and the money safely taken away, and then do the job on Lockridge if he was planning a double-cross?"

I gave him the theory I had conceived in the hospital. "It's pretty isolated up there in the hills, Eb. A body wouldn't necessarily be found for some time." I went on to tell him why it could be that this hypothetical silent partner had not waited until I was gone before killing Lockridge—that he had gotten excited by the prospect of the money, made his attack too quickly and merely wounded Lockridge with the first thrust of his knife instead of killing him, thus giving him time to cry out and warn me of what was happening.

"It makes sense, I suppose," Eberhardt said, but his voice was skeptical.

Donleavy said, "Yeah, it's pretty thin, all right—but it's better than anything else we've got at the moment. The only trouble with it, we don't have any goddamned idea where to begin looking for a silent partner." He sucked in his cheeks and puffed them out, the way he had in the hospital. "The girl didn't give you anything at all on a connection between Lockridge and somebody else out here?"

"Nothing," Eberhardt said. "As far as she knows, Lockridge conceived and executed the whole thing himself."

Donleavy yawned and patted his mouth the way Oliver Hardy used to do it; all he needed was a derby hat and a wide silk tie and a little mustache under his nose. He said, "Why do you suppose Lockridge brought the girl into it? It doesn't figure that she was part of any conspiracy, if there is one—and from what you told me over the phone, she only knew it was a kidnapping when Lockridge took the boy to the San Francisco house."

"Well, she said she was in love with the guy," Eberhardt said. "Maybe it was reciprocal, and he felt he could trust her. Maybe he figured it would be better to have somebody with the kid the whole time, and thought she was too dumb to tumble to the kidnap idea."

"I guess we'll never know about that now," Donleavy said sadly. "It doesn't figure this silent partner—again, if there is one—knew about her."

"I'd say it was pretty unlikely."

We kicked around what Lorraine Hanlon had told Eberhardt and me for a little while, and then Donleavy sighed and got up on his feet again. He went to the desk and put the phone bug in his pocket; the way he was handling it, he had already gone over it for prints—and the fact that he had not mentioned that, told me there had been none. He yawned again and looked at me and said, "Martinetti told me he'd hired you to do some investigating on this business. You planning to keep on with it now the boy is home?"

"If he still wants me, and you don't object, I guess I will," I told him.

"I figured as much," Donleavy said. "You seem to be all right, and you've been on this thing from the start; that's why I let you sit in just now. I can trust you to notify the office if you come up with anything, can't I?"

"Yes."

"Well, you've got my sanction then. I need all the help I can get." He said the last without irony.

There was a knock on the door, and Donleavy went over and opened it and spoke in low tones to a thin guy with a brushlike mustache. Then he shut the door again and came back and said, "That was one of the men I sent out to scout the area. None of the neighbors remember anybody hanging around before the snatch or after it; they turned up exactly nothing."

He puffed out his lips and sighed and looked at Eberhardt. "Do me a favor, would you? Ring up your Hall and see if Reese is still there?"

Eberhardt made the call for him, and Reese had not left as yet. Donleavy spoke to him, briefly, and put the receiver down and said, "I'm going to talk to the Hanlon girl myself, if you don't mind. Reese has a tendency to be too eager in his questioning, and he overlooks things; besides that, I like to be in on it first-hand. I told him to wait for me to get there."

Eberhardt inclined his head. "Listen," he said, "can I ride up with you? Hot shot here probably wants to talk to his client, and I got to get back."

"Glad to have you," Donleavy said.

We left the study then, without having reached any conclusions or made any startling discoveries after the revelation of the phone tap. It was just like most police work: a lot of conjecture, a little bullshit, and a constant rehashing of pertinent facts. Sometimes you clicked on something, and sometimes you didn't; but it was time well spent, because in the long run that was the way most cases were solved.

17

After Eberhardt and Donleavy had said their goodbyes to the Martinettis, I went with them out to the street. It was dark now, and very cool and still; the night air contained the faint, almost anachronistic presence of woodsmoke. It was a nice evening, all right.

I asked Donleavy, "When are you going to release the news of the boy's homecoming to the press?"

"Later on tonight, probably, after I have a talk with the Hanlon girl."

"Don't worry," Eberhardt said. "We'll see that you get the hero's mantle, hot shot."

"Oh, thanks," I said.

They got into the dark brown Ford—the Plymouth was gone, now—and Donleavy took it away up the street. I watched it turn right at the first corner and leave Tamarack Drive empty and silent again.

I retraced my steps across the footbridge and

through the gate. I was conscious of a gnawing sensation in my stomach now, but it had nothing to do with the knife wound; I had eaten nothing all day except a couple of pieces of toast while I waited for the taxi this morning. After I talked with Martinetti, I decided I would drive into Burlingame and get something to eat before returning to San Francisco.

I went along the gravel path, and Martinetti was on the terrace, at the outdoor bar, motioning to me. I angled across the lawn on the circular stepping stones and walked across the terrace to where he was standing. The drapes across the bay window were parted in the center, and as I passed by I could see Karyn Martinetti still sitting on the couch with her son. I could not tell if they were alone, or if Proxmire was in there with them.

Martinetti had a tall, thin glass in his hand, filled with a darkly amber liquid. He raised it slightly as I reached him, and said, "Would you like a drink?"

"I don't think so," I said. "Not just now."

He sat on one of the leather-topped stools and leaned his elbows on the marble surface of the left-hand bar face, rolling the glass distractedly between his palms. He did that for a time, and then turned his head and looked at me somberly. He said, "Will you continue working for me now?"

"If you like, Mr. Martinetti."

"Yes. Yes, I'd appreciate it."

"I'll do what I can."

He looked at his glass again. "I'd better tell you something, then," he said. "I didn't tell Donleavy or the other investigator this, but I suppose somebody should know. It's . . . a little painful."

I waited, not speaking.

He took a full, tired breath and put his eyes back on my face. He said, "Dean Proxmire is having an affair with my wife."

The surprise in my expression was due to his blunt admission of the fact, his knowledge of it, and not to the fact itself. I had considered telling Donleavy myself about the affair, what I had overheard the night of the ransom drop, but I hadn't done so simply because it seemed purposeless to air a lot of dirty linen unless it was absolutely necessary. Apparently Martinetti, at this point, felt it more necessary than I did.

I said awkwardly, because it was the thing to say, "Are you certain of that, Mr. Martinetti?"

"Yes." He raised the drink and swallowed some of it and ran his tongue over his lips with the open-mouthed carelessness of a toothless old man. "I've known about it for some time. Months, in fact."

"How long has it been going on?"

"Almost a year now, I think."

"And you haven't done anything about it in that time?"

"What would I do?" he asked. "Confront them with the knowledge, like an indignant cuckold? No, I'm afraid not. Karyn and I have been . . . out of love for a long, long time now. We haven't shared the same bed in more than a year. The only reason we've stayed together at all is because of the boy."

I was beginning to feel increasingly uncomfortable in this kind of discussion, but it was necessary enough from an investigative standpoint. I said, "You could have fired Proxmire."

"Would that have ended the affair?"

"I suppose not."

"The fact of the matter is, I'm a practical man," Martinetti said. "I'm also a relatively virile man, I think, and I understand the biological urge very well; I've had a number of casual affairs myself this past year, frankly. Why should I deny Karyn her release?"

That was what the progressive liberals referred to as being "the modern outlook." My uneasiness gained magnitude, and I did not speak.

"Besides that," Martinetti went on, "Proxmire is an extremely capable secretary. From a purely selfish point of view, it was simply easier to keep him on as long as he performed his duties as well as he has."

I looked over at the quiet blue-green water in the pool for a moment. A couple of eucalyptus leaves were floating on its surface like miniature canoes in a placid Lilliputian lake. I said at length, "Why are you telling me this now, Mr. Martinetti? Do you suspect Proxmire of having something to do with the death of Lockridge and the theft of the ransom money?"

"Not exactly," he said. "I will admit that the idea has crossed my mind a couple of times, because I know how much he wants Karyn—and Gary, too, for that matter; I can tell it by the way he looks at the boy—and the only thing keeping him from them is money."

"How long has he worked for you?"

"About a year and a half now. Why?"

"Then you should know him pretty well by this time," I said. "Is he the kind of man who would conspire to commit murder to obtain what he doesn't have?"

"Any man is capable of murder," Martinetti said quietly, "if he's pushed far enough, tempted strongly enough. A man is capable of a lot of things—and murder is one of them, just one of them."

"That doesn't answer my question, Mr. Martinetti."

"That's the best answer I can give you."

"You just said yourself that Proxmire had strong feelings for Gary. Would he jeopardize the boy's life by engineering a hijack of the ransom money? Would he risk the happiness, the completeness, of the woman he supposedly loves on the off chance—and that's all he could expect it to be—of the police finding Gary unharmed after the kidnapper was disposed of?"

Martinetti drank again from his glass, deeply this time. "I don't know," he said. "It's possible, isn't it?"

"I suppose it is."

"That's the only reason I mentioned it at all."

"Would you like Proxmire to be guilty?" I asked him.

His smile was faint and sardonic. "In a way, I suppose I would. In another way, for Karyn's sake, I hope he isn't."

"And if he isn't, do you intend to allow this situation to go on indefinitely?"

"Our little triangle, do you mean?"

"Yes."

"Well, I don't think I'll have to make a decision, either way. Karyn will be the one to do that, and I doubt if it will be very long before she does—especially after all that's happened in the past few days. If she loves Proxmire enough, and I suspect that she might now, she'll ask me for a divorce and custody of the boy."

"Will you agree to that?"

The faint and sardonic smile again. "Is that relevant to your investigation?"

"No," I said. "I'm sorry."

He made a dismissive gesture and drained the last of his drink without saying anything. There was the sound of a glass door sliding open, and Proxmire came out on the terrace. "Allan Channing just phoned," he called to Martinetti. "I told him about Gary, and he'll stop by for a few minutes on his way to San Jose."

"All right," Martinetti said.

Proxmire retreated into the house. I said, "If you don't mind, Mr. Martinetti, I'll be going now."

"You don't want to be here when Channing arrives, do you?"

"Not particularly."

"I can understand that, after the call he made to you this morning."

"You know about that?"

"He told me about it," Martinetti said, "after he'd made it. I told him he was a damned fool, for all the good it did. He's a very rich man, but he's also a very opinionated and very selfish man. He doesn't know how to handle relationships, except on a strict money-making basis."

"Yeah," I said.

"If it were possible for a man to have an orgasm looking at a bundle of money, I think Allan Channing would be that man." Martinetti laughed hollowly. "It would be nice if you could sit down and choose your friends according to your own ideals—or the ideals of society. But you can't do that, can you?"

"No, I guess you can't."

He stood up. "Well, to hell with all that. This is too pleasant an occasion for sober philosophical reflections. Do you want to come in and say goodbye to Karyn and the boy?"

"Yes."

We went into the house again, and I shook hands with Gary and with Proxmire, and stood with a sense of embarrassment that had no real foundation while Karyn Martinetti kissed my cheek a second time and thanked me again for finding her son. Then Martinetti and I walked out onto the front path.

He said, "Will you be by tomorrow? I should be here all day."

"I think so," I said. "I'll call you."

"I can give you a check for what I owe you then, if that's all right."

"Fine."

We said a parting, and I went away along the path and through the gate and out to where the Valiant was parked, lonely and somewhat tawdry in the lush quiet of Hillsborough. I felt very tired now; it was almost eight o'clock, and I had done a lot of moving around on this day —more moving around than a man should do with twenty-seven stitches in his belly. My legs were weak, and my neck was stiff and my head ached in a faintly annoying sort of way. I thought that after I had something to eat I would go straight home and get into bed. Tomorrow I would have to go down to some doctor or other and have the knife wound checked and the bandages changed; maybe I would have him give me a chest X-ray while he was at it, there was no sense in putting that off any longer.

I sighed very softly and tasted the aroma of the woodsmoke again, and then I went over to the Valiant. "You and me both," I said, and got inside and took it out of there.

18

I parked in front of the first café I saw in Burlingame, went inside and ordered some coffee and soup and a mound of creamed cottage cheese with fresh fruit; after I had put all of that away I felt considerably better.

The thought of a cigarette came into my mind then, and to get rid of it I got up from the counter and went back to where a telephone booth was located between the rest-room doors. I put a couple of dimes in the slot, the price of a Peninsula toll call, and dialed Erika's number.

She came on after a moment, and I said, "Hi, doll."

"Oh," she said, "hello, old bear."

She sounded vaguely cold, vaguely distant, and I thought: Oh Christ, she's still brooding over last night. Well, I was in a pretty decent frame of mind at the moment and I was not going to let one of her moods spoil it. I said, "I've got some good news. I found Gary Martinetti today—mainly through some blind luck. He's all right and safe at home with his parents."

"*You* found him?"

"Uh-huh." I told her how it had come about.

She said, "Well, that's very nice."

"Is that all you've got to say?"

"What would you like me to say?"

"You could show a little enthusiasm."

"For the boy—or for you?"

"Jesus, what's the matter with you tonight?"

"Not a thing, I'm fine."

"You don't act like it."

"I told you, I'm fine."

I sighed inaudibly, and said, "All right. Listen, I should be back in San Francisco in about half an hour. I'll come by and pick you up, and we can have a couple of drinks at my place before I go to bed—"

"No, I'm sorry," she said.

"What?"

"I'm sorry, I can't."

"Why not?"

"I'm going out pretty soon."

"Out where?"

"To dinner and cocktails."

"By yourself? Christ, Erika—"

"No," she said, "not by myself."

The back of my neck felt a little cold. "With who, then? Some other guy?"

"I don't think that's any of your concern."

"The hell it's not! You're supposed to be my girl."

"You don't own me," she said. "I can go where I please, with whom I please."

"What is this?" I said, and my voice was thick. "The goddamn brush-off or something? Is that it? If it is, you'd better tell me, Erika."

"Maybe it would be best that way," very softly.

"*Why*, for God's sake?"

"You know why. I told you why last night."

"Damn it, you're being unreasonable . . ."

"I don't think so. I thought it all out very carefully today, and I don't think I am."

"Erika, you know how I feel about you. Isn't that enough? What the hell do you *want* from a man?"

"That's just it: I want a *man*. Not a stubborn and self-deluding adolescent trying to live the life of a fictional hero."

"That's a plain bunch of crap!"

"No it isn't," she said. "You'd better resign yourself to the fact that you can't have that job of yours and me both. You're going to have to choose between us, one or the other."

"That's a hell of an ultimatum to offer a man!"

"I'm sorry, that's the way it has to be. I don't want to see you for a while, until you make up your mind. When you bring my car back, you can just park it in the driveway and put the key in my mailbox."

"Just like that, huh? Cold and reasonable, huh?"

"Yes."

"What about this bastard you're going out with tonight? Is that supposed to help me make up my mind, knowing you're out with somebody else?"

"He's not a bastard, and I'm going out with him because I don't intend to sit home and wait for your decision—not when I'm pretty sure I know how you'll choose."

"All right then!" I yelled at her. "All right then, go out with whoever you want and go to bed with him, too, for all I care, get yourself good and laid, goddamn it, I hope you—"

"Goodbye, old bear, I'm sorry," she said, and then she was gone and I stood there holding the phone like a dummy, panting, my face flushed and the nourishment I had just taken souring in my stomach. What was the matter with her, what the hell was the *matter* with her? Why couldn't she understand, why couldn't she empathize, didn't she know how it was with a man and the work he had to do? For Christ's sake, I loved her! I loved her, why wasn't that enough?

I slammed the phone back in its cradle and went out of the booth and threw some money on the counter. Outside, the wind blew cool and soft along the street and the black robe of the night sky was sequined with coldly bright stars. I began walking, just walking, letting the anger build, the frustration, letting it spiral inside me, and I thought: Well, all right, Erika, I'm glad to find out now the way it really is with you, how you really feel about me. I came within a couple of inches of dying the other day, and instead of coming to me like a woman with love and compassion in your words and in your eyes, you rub acid in the wound, you jump on me with your claws unsheathed like a predatory cat, "Goodbye, old bear, I'm sorry." Some succor, some understanding, some love— well, all right then, Erika, all right if that's the way you want it that's the way it will be, all right.

I kept on walking, and there was a cigar store on the opposite corner. I went over there and bought a package of cigarettes before I knew what I was doing, trance-like, but when I came out again with the pack in my hands, the spiraling had ascended to an ultimate zenith and there was nowhere else for it to go then but sharply downward. The anger vanished, and suddenly there was only a harsh, vacuous depression, a loneliness at the core of my soul that was almost painful in its fervor. But I did not want to be where people were, for it was not that kind of loneliness; it was, instead, the loneliness of rejection, the deep bleeding hurt of frustrated denial that only a woman can inflict upon a man.

There was nowhere for me to go. Home—the sanctuary? No, because home was the symbol of loneliness now, and the fragile lingering aura of Erika would be there and I did not want to be anywhere that reminded me of her, I did not want her car or her words whispering echo-like in my mind and the remembered feel of her softness beneath my hands and beneath my body.

I looked at the cigarettes and I did not want one at all, and I wondered fleetingly if I had bought them as a subconscious defiance of Erika. I dropped the package into my overcoat pocket and started walking again.

I walked for blocks and crossed streets blindly and walked, and finally my legs began to ache and my belly began to ache and I knew that I could not walk much longer. I needed something tangible to hang on to, something to do, someone to talk to, perhaps, something, anything, to take my mind off Erika. I started along an unfamiliar block, cutting back to the main street off which I had somehow strayed, and in the middle of it I passed a storefront with a wide display window illuminated by a single large-wattage night light. Black letters printed on the glass read *Books*.

I stopped. Inside the window, hanging from twine strung between pegs the width of the display, overlooking the pocketbooks and encyclopedias and other dusty second-hand items like tired and aged sentries on sagging battlements, was a series of pulp magazines—something tangible, something immediate, a second and fittingly ironic defiance of Erika because of her strong contempt for them.

I went up to the window and peered in at the magazines. You did not find many stores that had pulps any more, and I could see immediately why this one was an exception. There were some strips of paper clipped to the upper corners of the front covers, and on them were prices; the cheapest of the ones displayed was ten dollars and that was too much for anything except a vintage *Black Mask* or a Volume One, Number 1.

There were a couple of *Weird Tales* up there from the early forties, and an *Argosy* for 1936 and two copies of *The Shadow* from the late 1940's. I was not particularly interested in any of those, but there was a rare, fairly good edition of *Detective Fiction Weekly* for March 14, 1931, that caught and held my eye.

The distinctive dark blue-and-yellow cover depicted a detective who looked a little like Jimmy Stewart, throwing down on a heavy with a vial of something in his hand. Midway below the title, on the left-hand side, was a caption for the issue's feature story, *The Candy Kid*, a Lester Leith novelette by Erle Stanley Gardner.

The Lester Leith stories, about one of Gardner's earliest and most flamboyant detectives, were hard to come by these days in their original magazine appearance. They had been some of the best work of a master craftsman who had learned his trade in the pulps; Gardner had had a reputation in the old days

Gardner had had

Gardner

Gardner.

Gardener.

Oh Jesus, gardener—the *gardener!*

The impact of the connection was strong and sharp in my mind, and suddenly I had something else to grasp, something potentially important, something pushing Erika and the hurt and the depressing loneliness away.

Burlingame Landscaping and Gardening Service.

Very clearly, then, I could see the green panel truck behind which I had parked that first afternoon on Tamarack Drive—the words stenciled across its rear doors. And I could see the young T-shirted guy kneeling on the strip of canvas, weeding the lawn, when I first entered the grounds—the gardener, one other person who could have known about the kidnapping of Gary Martinetti the day it happened, who could even be the hypothetical silent partner acquainted with the Martinettis well enough to set up things for Lockridge—the gardener, the damned gardener.

I turned away from the window and hurried up the street, thinking that I had to get in touch with Donleavy, wondering if he was still up in San Francisco at the Hall of Justice—but before I reached Broadway, I slowed down and some of the urgency left me. It was nothing, for God's sake, but a shot in the dark, a fat straw, a possibility that was no better than any or all of the other possibilities. For all I knew, Donleavy or one of the other investigators from the District Attorney's Office had already questioned the gardener and eliminated him as a suspect; Donleavy would not necessarily have mentioned it in my presence. Even if they had not questioned him, I had no evidence against the gardener, nothing to link him with the kidnapping or the hijacking, nothing at all which would induce

Donleavy to drop his investigation of the sixty or seventy people who had been at Martinetti's party two nights before the boy's abduction—people who were just as suspect —and rush out to the gardener's place to interrogate him.

But it was still a lead, I could not deny that, and because it was—because I still needed that something tangible to hold on to, that weapon to ward off the loneliness —I could follow it up myself. Martinetti was paying me to investigate, and Donleavy had given me his blessings, if I needed any rationalizations—why not? If I learned anything of importance, then I could get in touch with Donleavy and let him take it over.

I began hurrying again, onto Broadway, along it to the café where I had eaten. In the phone booth at the rear, I opened the Peninsula directory; under the B section I found:

Burl Lndscp & Grdng Srv
87 Valldemar Dr (Bg) 344-1134

I shut the book and went out to the Valiant and rummaged in the glove compartment until I found a series of maps I knew Erika kept in there, bound with a rubber band. I located the one for the San Francisco Peninsula and looked up Valldemar Drive.

It was on the western edge of Burlingame, near Cuernavaca Park. That was a residential area, and it seemed logical to assume that whoever the young guy was, he ran his gardening and landscaping service from his residence.

The steering wheel had the feel of Erika's fingers on it as I drove away into the night.

19

Valldemar Drive turned out to be two blocks of split-level and ranch-style development homes, with a lot of trees and flowers and well-thought-out landscaping. Number 87 was of the former type, constructed of redwood with a fieldstone façade, and there was a large horse chestnut tree growing in a carpetlike front lawn to set it off somewhat from its neighbors.

I parked just off the curving front drive and got out and went up onto the sidewalk. At the foot of the drive there was a black metal pole with a carriage-type gas lamp on top of it; pale electric light shone through the cut-glass sides. An iridescent plastic sign in a wrought-iron frame was fastened to the center of the pole; *The Shanleys*—and below that, *Peggy and Glen*—was imprinted there.

The drive was bordered on the right with neat rows of yellow and white narcissus and lavender iris and pale pink gladiolas, and on the left by a low rough-hewn split-rail fence. At the back, parked in front of a darkened garage, was the green panel truck; there was no other vehicle in sight. I went along to where there was an opening in the fence, and a path made of variegated concrete blocks cut diagonally through the lawn, under the chestnut, and blended into a concrete porch covered with an arbor of honeysuckle. The fragrance of the vines' pale white flowers was rich and cloying in the cool night air.

I passed under the arbor and stepped up to the door. There was another gas lamp set on the wall beside it, this one dark, and below it I could see an ivory bell button. I pushed the button and stood there holding my hat in my left hand, trying to decide how I was going to handle things—and then the soft pad of footsteps sounded inside and a light came on in the lamp. The door opened and a woman looked out.

She was in her late twenties, tiny and compact, breasts a little large—pleasantly so—for the petiteness of her body, and a waist no thicker than a big man's thigh. She had one of these freckled pixie-ish noses that would wrinkle up like a rabbit's when she laughed, and carelessly fluffed hair the color of burnished copper, and large, innocent, gold-flecked green eyes. A bulky beige sweater and black flare slacks and a frilly apron with large heart-shaped pockets comprised her dress.

She asked quizzically, "Yes? May I help you?"

"Mrs. Shanley?"

"Yes?"

"I'd like to speak to your husband, if I may."

"Oh, well, I'm afraid he's gone to San Jose," she said. "His lodge is holding some sort of bowling tournament down there. Was it something to do with business?"

"Not exactly," I said. I got my wallet out of my

suit coat and opened it and let her look at the photostat of my operator's license. "I wanted to ask him some questions concerning the kidnapping of Louis Martinetti's son."

She blinked rapidly, and her mouth became a small, moist circle. "You're that detective in the newspapers, the one who was stabbed, aren't you?"

I nodded. She seemed a little awed, and her eyes moved down to my stomach, as if she expected to see blood there—or gaping flesh; then she blinked again and brought her gaze back up to my face. "Such a terrible thing, a kidnapping," she said gravely. "An awful, evil thing. Has there been any news yet?"

"As a matter of fact, there has," I told her. "Good news. The boy has been found, unharmed, and he's home with his parents at the moment."

The gravity gave way to a gladsome smile, and her freckled little nose wrinkled exactly the way I had thought it would. The relief in her eyes appeared to be authentic. "I'm so relieved!" she said. "Did the police arrest anyone?"

"A woman accomplice."

"A *woman* murdered that man and stabbed you?"

"I don't think so, Mrs. Shanley."

"Oh. Do you know who did yet?"

"Not yet, I'm afraid."

"Well, at least the boy is safe and that's the main thing, isn't it?"

"Yes."

She took her lower lip between her teeth and nibbled on it and put her hands in the pockets of her apron. "I suppose you want to ask Glen a lot of routine questions," she said. "He's been sort of expecting it."

"Why is that, Mrs. Shanley?"

"Isn't that the way it's done?" she asked. "I mean,

don't you investigators go around to everyone who knows or works for the victim in a case like this and try to find clues?"

"Yes, that's usually the way it's done."

"Glen is a good citizen," Mrs. Shanley said firmly. "He's always willing to cooperate with the authorities."

"That's good to know."

"Yes. I don't think he can be of much help, though."

"Why do you say that?"

"Well, when he came home the night that poor little boy was taken and told me about it, I asked him a million questions and he couldn't tell me anything at all."

"He knew about the kidnapping the day it happened?"

She inclined her head vigorously. "It was his day to work at the Martinettis'—he goes there once a week, in the afternoons—and he happened to be weeding under the study windows, you see, when Mr. Martinetti and that friend of his, Mr. Channing, were talking inside about what had happened. Glen isn't the type to eavesdrop, but, well, you don't just walk away when you hear something like that, do you?"

"No, I suppose you don't," I said. "I wonder if you'd mind telling me if your husband was home the following night, Mrs. Shanley? The night I was attacked and the kidnapper murdered."

"Yes, certainly he was. We watched television for a while, and then some friends came over for drinks and we played canasta until after midnight."

"Do you know if your husband told anyone else about the kidnapping that first day?"

"I don't think he did." She frowned thoughtfully.

"We didn't go out that night either, and no one dropped by . . . Oh, he might have told Art, I guess. Art telephoned about something just before supper and they talked for quite a while; I was in the kitchen, and I didn't hear any of the conversation."

"Who would Art be, Mrs. Shanley?"

"Glen's brother. He lives in Half Moon Bay."

"Anyone else he might have told?"

"Not that I know of," she answered. "Glen said that it was the kind of thing you didn't want to go spreading around, and he told me not to say anything about it."

"And you didn't, of course."

"Oh no."

I turned my hat around in my fingers. "Would your husband happen to have an interest in electronics, Mrs. Shanley?"

"Electronics?"

"Yes."

"Do you mean stereo equipment?"

"Generally, yes."

"Glen isn't very interested in things like that, really," she said. "His only hobby is his work."

"I see."

"But Art fools around with stereo equipment," she said. "He's built a couple of things from component kits or whatever you call them. Why do you ask?"

I rubbed at the bridge of my nose. "No special reason," I said noncommittally. "Would you happen to have your brother-in-law's address, Mrs. Shanley? You did say he lived in Half Moon Bay?"

"Yes," she said. "He has an ocean-view cottage on Dreyer Road—that's a little winding lane a couple of miles south of the village; there are only two cottages at the end of the lane, and his is the nearest one at the fork."

"What does he do for a living?"

"Well, he's unemployed at the moment. Usually he works as a plumber's helper, but there's been such a building depression lately that he can't find work."

"All right, Mrs. Shanley," I said. "Thank you for your time. You've been very cooperative."

"I'm afraid I didn't have much to tell you," she said. "Will you still be wanting to talk with Glen?"

"It's very likely," I said. "I'll be by tomorrow—or perhaps one of the District Attorney's investigators instead."

"He should be home until about noon," Mrs. Shanley said. "He doesn't have an appointment until one o'clock."

"Thanks again, Mrs. Shanley," I said, and managed a small smile for her and then turned around and went out to the street again. I sat in the darkness inside the Valiant and thought: Well, what have you got now? A brother who dabbles in electronics like a million other people in this country, who is unemployed like a few million others on top of that, and who may or may not have known about the kidnapping the same day it happened. That's all you've got, too, because if that girl was lying about her husband being home with her the night of the hijack, she's as good as Hepburn and twice as good as Taylor.

So what now? A talk with Art Shanley? Well, you've got nothing better to do tonight, and no place better to go than Half Moon Bay, because home is no more appealing than it was a little while ago. If it's a dead end, then you've made a full cycle out of it and you'll have something to report to Donleavy and Martinetti in the morning, even if it is negative.

I sat there awhile longer, thinking, but Erika came into my thoughts with her whispering words and her softness and her rejection, and abruptly I started the car and put the heater on high; it had grown very cold in there.

I drove over to Skyline Boulevard, and it took me fifteen minutes to make the nine-mile drive across the mountains to Half Moon Bay. I turned into one of the service stations at the Highway 1 junction there, got gas for the Valiant, and went into the attendant's office to look at a posted area map on the wall. Dreyer Road was a thin black line extending erratically south in a rough parallel to Highway 1; it began on Cliffside Drive, a road which right-angled seaward off the highway about three miles south, and according to the map scale, dead-ended less than a mile after it commenced.

I went out and paid the attendant and turned south, passing on the outskirts of the village of Half Moon Bay—a small cluster of buildings huddled seaward like old ladies under the tattered gray shawl of the coastal fog. The mist, which had been thick and fleecy on the road coming over, was higher and thinner here at sea level. It made the highway as slick as polished black glass under my tires and headlights, and spotted the windshield with the kind of liquidity you get from an aerosol spray can.

The section of the coastline beyond the village was barren and sparsely populated. To the left, undeveloped and thinly vegetated land stretched away into the wet gray-black of the night; to the right, the soil was rocky and grown with cypress and eucalyptus in a kind of windbreak well removed from the road. Deep, slope-sided, element-eroded ravines split the high cliffs overlooking the Pacific in hundreds of places, some of them extending inland as far as half a mile. You could see the lashing assault of the wind-swept sea on the jagged rocks from certain spots along the highway, but at others your vision was cut off by the trees and the rocky terrain and you were as much as a mile from the ocean itself.

I knew the area a little; there were a few homes and cottages strung out on the bluffs, or set back along the sides of the ravines—man-made blemishes on the awesome face of nature. Most of them had access to narrow strips of driftwood-strewn beaches along winding paths down the steep gorge slopes. It was in one of these dwellings that Art Shanley apparently lived.

I reached Cliffside Drive and turned off and followed its narrow, pitted expanse past a few lighted homes and a lot of wet, shiny ice plant that was greenly opalescent in the diffused radiance from my headlamps. A quarter-mile in, a wooden sign loomed on the left and the words *Dreyer Rd.* were visible on it in small black lettering. I swung down there, and it was nothing more than a graveled cart track winding in a southwesterly direction, hugging and skirting two of the shallower ravines without any sign of habitation. Then the road straightened out onto a fog-shrouded bluff face, and split into two forks. There was a lot of thickly bunched scrub oak and cypress growing in the crotch of the fork and paralleling the branch which wobbled its way further southwest and ended a few hundred yards distant at the vaguely discernible outlines of a darkened cottage. The second branch hooked back to where another cottage squatted dimly at the edge of the near ravine; that would be Shanley's, from what his sister-in-law had said. Bars of pale light shone through straight-louvered shutters over a long front window, glowing eerily through the shimmering wetness of the fog.

I turned the Valiant in that direction and coasted into a wide circle before it. A black or dark blue Rambler American, sheened with wetness and rust-scarred by the perpetually damp salt wind, was parked with its front wheels touching one of three logs which had been set as brakes thirty feet in front of the cottage. I parked beside it at a second log.

The building, I could see in the shine of the headlights, was weather-beaten pineboard, a dull eroded gray with a lot of humps and knots like a beachcomber's shack. It was enclosed in front by a similar board fence, and off on one side was a small matching shed. There was a look of instability to it all, as if a good stiff storm wind would hurl the cottage and the shed out over the cliffs and into the ocean.

I switched off the lights and got out of the car. Cold wind whistled in from the sea, eddying the fog like mildewed garlands around my head. The sound of the turbulent Pacific seemed unnaturally loud out here, as if the bluff were a tiny atoll and the ocean was all around it, hammering at it, chipping it apart and consuming it piece by piece, inexorably. I shivered a little and pulled the overcoat tight around my neck, moving quickly to the unlatched gate in the fence.

A crushed oyster-and-clam-shell path, grown through with coarse grass, extended into a wide rectangle before the door; on both sides of it, ice plant caressed the rough boarding of the cottage with shining green fingers. I went up to the rectangle and reached out and knocked on the door.

No answer. I waited half a minute, and then knocked again, listening for some sound from within. There was nothing except the stentorian and relentless roaring of the wind-lashed Pacific flinging itself on the rocks beyond and below.

I worked saliva into my mouth and took a couple of careful steps sideways, into the ice plant. My shoes crushed the wet pulpy tendrils with the same sound as when you step on a thick-shelled beetle. I leaned forward, retaining a breath, and put my eye up to one of the bars in the louvered shutters and looked inside the cottage.

A mélange of mismatched furniture—rattan, over-stuffed fabric, imitation Danish Modern—and the light coming from an inverted and milky-bowled floor lamp. Mail-order stereo components, all of which had apparently been built from kits, on tiers of shelves made out of brick building blocks and lengths of wood along one otherwise bare wall. A small wooden table cluttered with capacitors and resistors, solder and spools of wire and a soldering gun, various-sized parts and tools. Bare wood floor, a darkened archway to another room—nothing else. I touched my tongue to my cold lips and moved as far to the left as I was able so that I could see more of the room: more bare wall, a battered portable television set on a roll-stand, a cylindrical brass-finished smoking stand. The area immediately in front of the door was still blocked from my vision.

I stepped back onto the crushed-shell rectangle and knocked on the door a third time. Still nothing. Before I could consider the advisability of the move, I reached out and grasped the knob and twisted it slowly, silently. The door opened a couple of inches under my hand.

There was the smell of something in there, a lingering chemical odor that I had known a long time ago and would never forget: spent gunpowder. The hairs at the base of my neck rose, and a different kind of chill swept over me now; I could feel my heart begin to jump irregularly in my chest and there was sweat under my arms and flowing cold-hot along my sides. My stomach throbbed and ached.

I released the knob and pushed the door open with the tips of my fingers, keeping my body motionless. It swung inward with a faint, odd, empty sound, and then I could see the flooring across the threshold that had not been visible from the window.

A man lay on his right side there, a couple of feet into the room, facing away from me. His legs were drawn up, and both hands were frozen in clawed agony at his chest. Blood had spilled out between the spread fingers; a pool of it, with appendages as thin as spider's legs jutting out into the cracks in the boarding, shone a deep burgundy in the pale light.

I took a couple of steps inside, moving woodenly. The man was about thirty, dressed in faded corduroy trousers and canvas shoes and a white terry-cloth pullover with the word *Art* stitched in blue script over the left pocket. His face was contorted, the eyes squeezed so tightly shut they seemed sewn, and he had bitten through his lower lip in his agony.

I knelt down by his head and made myself look at his chest. It was a bullet wound, all right, but there was no sign of exit. I touched the skin at the base of his neck: still warm. He had not been dead very long.

I straightened up and kept on staring down at the thing that had been Art Shanley, undeniably Art Shanley, and I thought: He's the one, yes, he's got to be the one. He learned of the kidnapping from his brother and saw his chance to get his hands on more money than he'd ever seen before or would see again. He went down to Martinetti's late that same night and planted the bug in the phone and waited all the next day—maybe in his car, maybe just walking around with a portable radio—for the ransom call to come in. When it did, he went up to the drop site early and hid out there to wait for Lockridge, the kidnapper, and for me to show up with the money. But he was too quick after I put the suitcase on that sandstone rock, too nervous maybe, and he used the knife on Lockridge before I was gone. When I came back down, he slashed me and then got out of there with the money and he was in the clear—he *thought* he was in the clear.

I kept staring down at him, and the sight of his twisted features jarred my mind and suddenly I began thinking very clearly, very rationally, very rapidly. A lot of little things fused and grew and begat bigger things, and I began to tremble, standing there, tremble with more than mere coldness, the sound of the churning ocean growing and growing in my ears until it filled the room with crushing, cataclysmic noise. We had thought it all tied together, the kidnapping and the hijacking, but they were two separate entities, paralleling one another but never coming together until tonight. Now that I knew that, I knew also who had killed Art Shanley—who, and why, not all the answers, but enough of them, too many of them, and the knowledge made disgust flow through me with the palpable bitterness of camphor.

I turned away and let my eyes sweep the room, and there was a telephone on a black metal stand next to the bright-cushioned Danish couch. I went over and reached out for the receiver, and then I heard shuffling sounds from the darkness beyond the archway, strangely discernible above the deafening sea, and I realized that I had been a fool to come inside, a fool not to have considered the possibility that the killer was still on the premises, but it was too late now, too damned late, and when I pivoted he was there in the gloom beyond, with a gun held laxly in his right hand, a specter gaining substance as it moved into the light, stopping full-born and staring at me with the most terrible eyes I had ever seen—eyes that reflected all of man's most hellish nightmares.

I stood facing a swindler, a murderer—and worse, perhaps much worse: a man so merciless, so cruel, that he had arranged the kidnapping of his own son.

I stood facing what was left of Louis Martinetti.

20

The gun was a .32-caliber Smith and Wesson revolver, walnut-butted, with an almost nonexistent barrel—a belly gun that looked almost toylike in the largeness of Martinetti's hand. He held it half-turned, palm up at a forty-five-degree angle, and the bore of it pointed loosely at my lower body.

His face had the look of food mold in the dim light from the floor lamp, and his lips twitched and danced in a kind of macabre rhythm, like the muscle spasm of a dead man. The deep excavations were back beneath his cheekbones. But the eyes—oh Jesus, those eyes!—caught and held your own gaze, and even though you wanted to look away, look anywhere but into those diseased and frightening depths, you could not seem to do it. They were hypnotic, holding you mesmerized with all the horror they contained.

I stood rigidly, my arms pressed tight against my

sides, and I looked into those eyes and, curiously, I was not afraid. I should have known fear, because there was fear all around me in that room and because I was facing a gun that had already killed one man tonight—and yet, it was absent from my mind. I felt only a great despondency at the knowledge of what man can become, and an anger, too, and a nauseous disgust. I felt very tired, and very cold. But that was all—truly, that was all.

Neither Martinetti nor I spoke for a long time, and the thundering roar of the vast ocean swirled around us, reverberating, swelling the air in that room and swelling it until it seemed as if the pressure of the noise would burst the walls. And then it became no louder, as if waiting, as if maintaining that pitch like a great clarinetist would maintain the screaming high notes of Jelly Roll Morton's "Iceburg Blues," the power of it awesome and frightening but not as frightening as Martinetti's eyes.

I said the words that were thick on my tongue, "You son of a bitch."

He released a prolonged, sighing, shuddering breath and raised his left hand and passed it over the loose wetness of his mouth. "Yes," he said, and that single word was no more than a death rattle, all inflection abrogated by the consuming sound of the Pacific.

"What motivates you, Martinetti? What do you use for a conscience, for a soul? What *are* you, for God's sake?"

Something, a ghastly presence, came and went on his face. "I don't know," he said with a kind of sick wonder. "I don't *know!*"

"Your own son," I said. "Your own flesh."

"So simple in the beginning," he said, "not so terrible . . . intelligent boy, Gary, no emotional scars . . .

too stable, but it went wrong, there was no way it could go wrong, but it went wrong . . ."

I thought: Is this the actor worthy of an award, the coldly methodical mercenary, the bitterly vengeful cuckold? Is this the Louis Martinetti of chicanery and deceit and extra-legalities, of the forceful and magnetic personality—this shell, this decaying creature with the zombie eyes?

But I said, "It was the money, wasn't it, Martinetti? The three hundred thousand dollars of Channing's money. That's why you did it."

"The money," he said, "oh yes, I had to have the money . . . the real estate investment closing up and no more assets, no place to turn—Jesus God, it meant millions and Channing was the only one with the kind of cash I needed . . . Channing, that bastard, that cold bastard, never loaned a cent in his life, never bet on a long shot and so proud of it—well, I gave him something to shake his pride, didn't I? I gave him a kidnapping, I gave him a goddamn ultimatum—how would the newspapers like to know you refused to save a little boy's life, Allan? You think about that, you bastard . . ."

He stopped talking and stood there motionless. I could feel the sweat on my own body, as motionless as his. It was as if we had been frozen, solidified, in the tableau of the room—a scene of horror cast in wax at Madame Tussaud's. A half-minute passed and I got some saliva through the dry crust inside my mouth and I said, "Lockridge, Martinetti. What was your connection with Lockridge?"

"Lockridge," he repeated, and he kept standing there, rigid, the gun not moving in his hand. I counted to six before he spoke again, the words like those on a recording tape being played for the millionth time, words which had lost all their human qualities and become the expressions of a machine. "He didn't have a choice either, I told him that, I said not with your underworld connections there in Ohio—one word from me would have sent him to prison for a long time . . . oh no, I didn't have to give him fifty thousand, but it was my safety margin, all planned so carefully . . ."

Yeah, I thought, you planned it all so carefully. You must have met Lockridge in Ohio, your wife is from there, and maybe you used him in some capacity on your schemes and deals over the years; it figures that way. So when you came up with the kidnapping idea, you brought him out here and briefed him on the situation and told him about the area in the San Bruno hills to be used as a drop point. You told him to treat Gary with kid gloves, to buy some of his favorite books and models so that the boy would be comfortable, and you gave him Gary's exact clothing sizes, too, so that he wouldn't have to keep wearing his school uniform. Then you wrote out that kidnap note yourself, on your personal stationery, and signed your name to it; that's why the headmaster at Sandhurst never questioned the signature: it was authentic.

But you didn't know where Lockridge was holding Gary. You weren't acting after Lockridge was killed and I had been stabbed and the money hijacked. Maybe you were *supposed* to know where the boy was, maybe you thought you *did* know. You had to keep up the masquerade of waiting by the phone and so you couldn't get away to check on the boy until the following afternoon, probably just before you came to see me in the hospital; sure, and maybe you planned to keep Gary from seeing you somehow and then drop some clue to Donleavy or me later on. But then, if I'm guessing right, you discovered that the boy was not where he was supposed to be and you panicked; you weren't aware of the Hanlon girl—Lockridge had brought her in on his own, for his own reasons—and you thought Gary was alone, locked up somewhere, that he might starve to death if he wasn't found. Lockridge had pulled a fast one on you, an irony you never expected, either because he wanted some insurance that you kept your part of the bargain you'd made with him, or because he intended to hold you up for a larger percentage of the money. It doesn't matter now; it just doesn't matter at all.

The rest of it is simple enough to figure. You brought me into the kidnapping in the beginning because you needed a witness to the money exchange, a corroborator that a kidnapping *had* taken place, when you went to the police after you had the money and Lockridge was on his way back to Cleveland; Channing would have expected, demanded, that the affair be reported as soon as Gary was returned home. You asked me to keep working for you when the boy was still missing for just the reason you gave me in the hospital: you wanted all the men available looking for Gary. And you asked me to stay on tonight because it would not have seemed proper to dispense with my services after I had been the one to find your son; and perhaps because you wanted to punish your wife—and Proxmire—by having me question them about a possible complicity. That would be the reason, too, why you told me tonight about the affair between them.

All that remains, Martinetti, is the question of Art Shanley. When I talked to you that first afternoon in your study, you went to the drapes and looked out at the rear grounds; you must have seen the gardener—Glen Shanley—out there, and later assumed that he might have overheard something between you and me, or between you and Channing earlier. It's likely that you didn't make any connection at all at first, because you were too upset by the hijacking and then too concerned, in spite of it all, for Gary's safety. But once the District Attorney's man, Reese, found the phone bug—and once I reported locating Gary—you had time to think and remember seeing the gardener.

But how did you know about Glen Shanley's brother, Art, here in Half Moon Bay? Glen's wife would have told me if you had talked to her. Well, maybe Glen mentioned his brother at one time or another, also mentioned that Art dabbled in electronics, and you recalled that, extrapolated it. You couldn't have known for certain that Art Shanley was the hijacker, but you had a strong suspicion, and that was enough for you to come out here tonight . . .

I stopped talking mentally to Martinetti, watching him closely now. He seemed to be swaying slightly, like a frail and withered tree in a strong wind. He was no longer looking at me or even through me. He was looking *around* me to where the body of Art Shanley lay in its coagulating blood on the floor.

A sound that was something between a cough and a sob came from deep within him, perhaps from the very core of him. And he began talking again, in that same dead, unhuman voice. "I didn't want to do this, I didn't want to do this . . . I told him I'd give him fifty thousand and forget about what he'd done if he turned the rest of the money over to me, but he laughed, he laughed, he said that if he *was* guilty, and he was, I knew it then, oh, I could see it in his eyes, he said he would be a fool to accept that kind of offer. He tried to throw me out, he put his hands on me and we struggled and then I I I I just took the gun out of my pocket and I shot him, I shot him . . ."

Again he stopped talking. I said softly, "Do you remember what you said to me tonight, at your home, Martinetti? About how any man is capable of murder—and a lot of other things, too—if he's pushed hard enough, if he's tempted strongly enough? Well, maybe you were pushed and tempted that hard, just as this real estate thing tempted you into having your own son kidnapped. Maybe you wanted Shanley dead, even though you wouldn't admit it to yourself, because with him out of the way you were completely safe and you would have eliminated the man who caused you so much anguish, who almost killed your son and your chance to regain a lost fortune. Maybe you *did* intend to kill him all along. Why else the gun? Why else would you park your car in the trees by the road fork—that's where it is, isn't it?—instead of driving directly up to the cottage here? Why else did you shoot him?"

"Oh God," Martinetti whispered. "Oh God!"

"The money," I said. "Where's the money?"

The quivering of his lips had worsened now, and saliva glistened on them, welling at the corners like fat and obscene tears. "The suitcase, it was in the closet, I opened it and I looked at the money, all that money, and suddenly I didn't want it any more I didn't want it I didn't care about it I didn't want to see it, all I could see was him lying there in the dark, but the image of him wouldn't go away, I killed him . . . I murdered him . . ."

"Three hundred thousand dollars," I said half audibly. "The price of a soul."

"I'm a murderer," he said, "yes, I'm a murderer, I

killed him don't you know that? I murdered him murdered him murdered him . . ."

He kept on that way, softer and softer, the words becoming unintelligible to me, and he was speaking only to himself now, to the very essence of his being. He no longer knew I was there. He was a callous man, a hard man, a man who had been very close to crime, even to criminals, over the years, skirting the periphery of illegality and immorality, never really affected by it—and yet, he had never himself had to deal with the cold, terrifying fact of death, of murder, of the awesomeness of snuffing out a human life. Faced with the thing he had done, the circumstances which had led to the act—examining it within himself—he was unable to cope with it; it was destroying him so quickly and so completely that the effects of that destruction were outwardly visible.

As I listened to him babbling, I realized that he was totally incapable of pulling that trigger another time, of taking a second human life—and I realized, too, that I had known all along that this was true, that I had stood facing his gun not as a brave man facing death, but as a man who knows irrevocably the outcome of a situation, knows that he will not be harmed in any way. I looked deep into Martinetti's eyes and saw the terrible guilt, the cancerous insanity burning in their depths, and then I forced my gaze again to the gun in his hand. It was no longer pointing at me; the muzzle was angled toward the floor at my feet.

There were perhaps three steps between us, three long quick strides, and his shoulders were slumped now, muscles lax, mouth open to release his murmurings—three long quick strides. I took them without thinking any more about it and hit him the same way, a long hard right-hand flush on the point of his jaw, the shock of the impact exploding the length of my arm and into my armpit, pain through my knuckles, and he went down clean and silent, with his eyes rolling up in their sockets, sprawling out on top of the gun, covering it with his body, unmoving.

I stood looking down at him, breathing heavily. I felt nothing at all. The anger and the hatred and the disgust were gone now, and they had left nothing in their place but a hollow vacuum, a weariness that transcended the physical.

My hands were trembling and I thrust them into the pockets of my overcoat to still them, and the fingers of my right hand encountered the package of cigarettes I had bought earlier in the evening. I took it out and looked at it, and then I closed my eyes and tore open the pack and lit one and dragged smoke deep into my lungs. It was harsh and raw and hot and brought a vague weakness to my knees—it was fine.

I went over to the telephone and picked up the receiver and stood holding it, looking over at Martinetti lying very still, very old, like some crumbling sarcophagus. And, strangely, I thought then of Erika.

You were right, Erika, I thought. You were right that I'm honest and ethical and sensitive, that I don't have a lot of flair or even a lot of guts. You were right that I'm not a hero, and that I never will be.

But you were wrong, too. You said that I'm nothing more than a little boy playing at being a detective, that I'm living in the past, in a world that never existed. But the world I live in, you live in, is a world sicker and harsher and crueler than anything in man's imagination, a lousy world that requires men like Donleavy and Reese and Eberhardt to keep it from becoming sicker and harsher and crueler than it already is, dedicated men, Erika, men who care. I'm one of those men—how or why I got to be that way is of no real consequence—and because I am, I'm not living the lie you think I am.

You can't change me, Erika, you can't hope to make me into something that I'm not and never will be. And that's why, if I must choose, I won't choose you, even though I love you; I am what I am, and how can you cease being—how can you alter in any way—what you *are?*

I'm no hero.

I'm just a cop.

I'm just a man.

I sucked deeply, hungrily, on my cigarette and dialed the operator, and when she came on I asked her for the police above the tintinnabulation of the restless and eternal sea. . . .